We Defy Augury

THE FRENCH LIST

We Defy Augury

HÉLÈNE CIXOUS

Translated by Beverley Bie Brahic

LONDON NEW YORK CALCUTTA

The work is published with the support of the
Publication Assistance Programmes of the Institut français

Seagull Books, 2020

Originally published as Hélène Cixous, *Défions l'augure*
© Éditions Galilée, 2018

First published in English translation by Seagull Books, 2020
English translation © Beverley Bie Brahic, 2020

ISBN 978 0 8574 2 783 0

British Library Cataloguing-in-Publication Data
A catalogue record for this book is available from the British Library.

Typeset by Seagull Books, Calcutta, India
Printed and bound by Versa Press, East Peoria, Illinois, USA

Contents

Acknowledgements

I am grateful to Nicholas Royle, a fabulous writer and resurrectional reader of the literature I love, especially Shakespeare's, for having revived in the nick of time, in his *An English Guide to Bird-Watching, Hamlet*'s magico-tragic formula, 'We defy augury' (V. ii),

Affectionate thanks to Annie-Joëlle Ripoll and Fatima Zenati, whose vigilance gives me the peace to work.

Hélène Cixous

Acknowledgements are also due to Michael Schmidt, editor of *PN Review* 45(6) (July–August 2019), in whose pages the chapter titled 'You Never Know Who Is Going to Come In' was first published.

Beverley Bie Brahic

A Note from the Author

—Since your chest is aching and you have dark presentiments, don't go to battle, put it off, heed the auguries, when you feel that the end is near, back off as our good friend Horatio advised. Remember?

—Me? Back off? Never in your life! *We defy augury!* To be, Hamlet says, is to *defy augury*. I am, therefore I go. We have to live and live well, this time it has been decided. We mortals, that is the living, aren't we already close to Paradise, that is, *all ready* in the first instance *to lose it,* in order, in the second instance, to see it resurrect? this Book says. *The Readiness is all* as Shakespeare and Montaigne agree.*

This Book rehearses the dance with the augury. It is populated with splendid co-dying with splendid revenants and rebecomers, with comemorants, beloved beings lifted out of nothingness, come from all the worlds and continents, racing from one century to another, from Germany to Africa from South Africa to South America, from the Souths to the Norths and vice versa, defying oblivion, hoisting themselves out of effacement,

Warnings, presages, memories of catastrophes, signs, presentiments, dreams that delight in multiplying like the stars in Manhattan better viewed from the 107th floor of the World Trade Center than from Ground Zero, we are made to *take back life* wherever it has been cut off.

* Most of the phrases in English in the original are in italics here.—Trans.

As I see it, this Book is the incarnation of our turbulent lives. It is an assemblage of chasms and fêtes. Twenty times it gasps for breath, clambers over abysses and ruptures, falls below ground or at other times grows airy.

It may happen that I divine, behind my mother's hidden influence and her digressive genius, the fateful present-indelible of the immense Jonas family, from their first expedition on board the whale to the Bacharach Jonas tribe, and, following their flight, the Osnabrückers, folks who relocate in the space of a few hours or lines to a dozen scattered cities.

What's today? It's 2001 and also 1791. What a joy to be simultaneous! It's the magic gift for those who every second generation are expelled from their birthplaces. All is lost!? The Book invites us to regain Paradise. Let's find once more the Towers and those who've disappeared, the capital cities and the villages. No time for melancholy! Everything resuscitates intact. *Paradise means to come back.*

My books are the domain of Morpheus. My poets are all dead. The dead still live in the cities that yesterday they cast their spell over. Ghosts? my daughter asks. Time's guardians, I say.

A Note on the Text

'Where there is no punctuation at the end of a sentence or section, it is that those thoughts continue somewhere else, off the page [. . .] white spaces in the text correspond to the discontinuities of time and thought.'

Hélène Cixous Seminar
Cité Universitaire de Paris
16 March 2019

The 2020s—they were already on our mind the 20s twenty years ago yesterday, we were walking alongside Ground Zero, you were full of fear.

If there are no more months, no years, autumn with its red-vermilion-flecked yellow wings remains, as if there were but one eternal season for love's re-beginnings. The same autumn a year ago in Manhattan, the Holy City lost its beautiful teeth, we were heartsick, always the same warning you say, no need to write a poem,

I'm grimacing because I left my hat in the taxi, I can always get another one, I can't get another one

Will we meet again twenty years from now in the New World as usual in this one? you ask. The world on the serpent's back? I say. Or in another, I say, the one that I arrive in, I forget if it's by train or car, the land of your prehistory? The strange paradise that death does not enter. This sutumn with its red-flecked-yellow wings was in 2002, and in twenty years we would be saying how young we were in 2001 and how we can still imagine it, you were, as always, fearful, we were off to the Towers of horn and ivory and the streets shivered a little as we went by. It is desire's nature to occupy the entire landscape. Let us once again walk up Time's Fifth Avenue.

I am out walking with my son, out walking with Isaac, one can per-
fectly well be present on several levels at once, in the diverse seconds
of October's forever melancholy mood, seconds whose staying power
is incalculably deep

You've lost your hat? It's not the first time, remember? Already in
Chicago, while I was losing Thea, the endless draining of all my bloods,
the workmen with their Day-Glo butterfly-yellow-and-orange vests
printed with big letters, 2001 was weeping and there'd be twenty years
of weeping death unto death, and now I am out walking in 20 with my
son. He asks if I have news of you.

No, I say, it's strange, but despite the weather I always think of you
between six and midnight; between midnight and dawn I wait for you;
I still love you, my only love. Excuse me a moment, I tell my son, there's
something I have to do, it's urgent: suddenly, an absolute need to *call
you right now*, after all these years. Here? Right this minute.

The need consumes all of the All. What will you say? You think
I've forgotten you? Have I forgotten you *my lonely love*, I have my life,
I have someone else? Him? But he's my son!—That's not a reason!—
Is! Isn't! Love loves you alone. *Could I forget, my only love, to love thee.
Have I forgot my only love* have I forgotten? Love loves you alone *my
only lonely love*, felled by time's axe; can I cease loving my only love, I
still feel the sad happiness of having been so happy at the hour misfor-
tune struck. Have I forgot the unforgettable?

Times passes, alas, and I've forgotten your number. I think I remember, I try, I dial, where are you? At home? At work? At the Palace? At
the New School? I thrust two fingers down the throat of my memory

and grope, it's not easy, I think I feel a 4 or 9 or 6. It's ringing, I hear a voice, oh! Yes, that's your voice down there, speaking to a disciple, I hear your clear, young voice. But I didn't dial the number right, you don't hear me, I'm going to shout, you're going to push me away, you left me, my scars healed, I got used to life without you, but one word and the awful love returns like a tornado, I want my life back, ah! If you leave me again I couldn't bear the pain, I am in flames and terror, my son is waiting, I am out of time. Shall I stop calling him? All these years and I'm still so scared of a mortal rejection. How long does the flight of a Paris–New York dream-balloon last, so light so strong, so frail? You are so close, I am in a blaze of pain, frantically I search for Isaac's number, a dozen times I thumb through my contacts, finally I find a whole line of I's, but no, they are train times, not a single phone number in the lot, and egged on by despair I decide to see if my fingers remember what my tongue does not, and that's when *the communication is established*, but cut off, too late, you have left, and chagrin utters a scream that pierces space to find you down there in the bottom of the dream. This scream is so loud it rips the dream's envelope and drops my eviscerated self onto the sandy shore like a gutted fish. Long after waking, the cry is still crying like a fool at large in the deserted air. Such suffering! I hurt all over, I take a Doliprane, I don't sleep. Never before has a dream kidnapped my day. In broad daylight I have crossed to the other side

No, Isaac didn't leave you, Waking says; he is dead, that's why it's been years since you called him, whereas all you had to do to get to the other side was dial his number. The address is in *The Odyssey*, Canto XI, in the place Circe told you, on the Ocean's edge, at dawn in Aquitaine.

I need help. I call my daughter: a dream seized me like an eagle, I say. She listens, with sympathy. Returns to what she was doing. I call my son. —Like a falcon, I say. —I can't talk. Is it urgent? —No, I say. It's a blessing.

The cruelest Dream. And yet a blessing: this storm of reality, this searing pain that bears your name, this violent survival of the dead, this City cast in the fire, how not to celebrate it? Perhaps a book began like that? With an upheaval?

The book is called *Fête*. Do you like it, I say? —Fate? —Exactly. Fête Fate.

Neither memory nor forgetfulness, I suffer from a fit of absence of world, time becomes intermittent, a month can pass without me without him without him coming to see me in a dream, then the desert ending finally, he returns, I was on the point of us dying, you are tired and ill after your fatal accident, you are handsome and quieter than usual, I hope you aren't annoyed, I haven't been able to call you, one of us was cut off, nothing has changed, do you have time? Have you a few days before the dream ends? We could spend an hour together: in the cinema's cellars. But have we the right? If *cinema* is written *si n'aima*, you whisper. We have a right to the ruses of the great divided. Were it not for literature, the sick-unto-death would not have survived their Tristia. Impossible to bear so much death without insurmountable hardship, this is Nature's law. And the almost dead touch each other, kiss, after so much fasting of course you look bewildered, but all I have to do is sit myself down in front of you, plunge my eyes into yours, connect your extinguished gaze, you light up, you smile, you recognize me,

I take you in my arms, I press my lips to your forehead, you say nothing, dead, remembering.

A month goes by: no me no you no memory no forgetting then you come as if we had seen each other only yesterday. A yesterday that was anxious, nervous, tormented by nameless apprehensions, like dogs haunted by threats of death.

—Spaghetti? asks my daughter. Astonished.

—Spaghetti. A large serving. A big bowl. Pasta, et nada.

Had they hoped for a taste of joy it didn't happen. A little further along, their enormous grief awaited them. This was to be their final fête, though they didn't know it. Or maybe someone had an inkling, but who? But what? How to explain the aura that brooded over the table, I said to my son, maybe death was already with us in the Italian restaurant, the guest you can't shake off, a long time before the death, death turns up uninvited, secretes this awkwardness that explains the gloom in the room? Or could it be that the act of commemoration drops a veil over the scene years after it took place? I see them seated at a small round table with a big white tablecloth. No one else in the room? No one. It's strange. In Manhattan, near Gramercy Park. Had everyone been warned about the disquieting Presence, and fled, or maybe The Tale only had eyes for its hostages?

Spaghetti. In the aftermath I will never forget the last bowl, *a large portion*. I will forget the rest. Or rather I'll forget everything except for the spaghetti. Over time it has swelled and swelled. It has a secret life. The restaurant bathed in darkness. It really exists. It is empty. I have proof: I have the card in my Persian notebook. The name *Sal Anthony* across a sea of forget-me-not clouds, a bowl of pasta for the gods. So they knew, the gods. I said: "It exists." Perhaps it too is dead, the restaurant with its immortal dreams. It's the fate of all the places we went when we weren't yet able to divine the auguries. Perhaps we didn't want to?

It comes to me that if all these places, hotels, restaurants, airports, cities and castles, oceans are also dead, it is not that a hostile destiny seeks to efface all our traces on this earth. Rather, the spirits that gave life to these scenes that were our tender allies have accompanied us to the secret present of the Other Side.

Afterwards, the Tale notes, she had trouble eating pasta. She feels as if she is taking food from his mouth. It's his spaghetti. Just before the hunger ends.

—The day I will be able to say why I don't write, my son says, I will be able to say why you do write, and this day being effaced I'll be effaced along with it, a thought and a certitude that transport me, my son says. —Madness, I say. But whose?

The idea of effacement unhinges me; I fear She'll rob me of my memory, Miss Insidious, whom I don't see, this shadow that, not being here yet, is all the more terrifyingly here and, word by word, raids my life and debits my brain. Mockingly she pilfers from me, a thief according to the law of anythinggoes. I am pillaged, of trinkets. If only she raided "Victor Hugo" but she robs me of the moniker of that celebrity, notoriously bewitching to men but whose blonde charm leaves me indifferent, does nothing for me but whose seizure promptly gives her the glamour of a tabloid titbit.

There's a Shadow. I don't see it. I don't sense it. It's a hypothesis. It's a sickness. An artful sickness, a poisoning of the powers of the imagination. Ever since death deprived me, in part, of Isaac, of his external self, I fear being infected by the sickness of fear. From this I deduce that Isaac was my invulnerability, thus my vulnerability, my mental armor, thus my lack of steel-plating. I fear losing the formula for immortality. Isaac believed I had the formula, therefore I had it.

Belief is what it takes to keep life alive.

All it takes is an accident, a breakdown of belief, a second's inattention, a nano-second, and Paradise is Lost, between one second and the next my mother let go. Perhaps my belief was broken. Perhaps the penultimate minute had been poised for a while.

What scares me is not knowing the exact hour of the last minute. Next week I might take a tumble in the staircase. I've tripped on a step, the cat Philia was underfoot, rather than killing her I flung myself against the wall, and that's how I lost my life. Death by cat, why not, that's one way. Or my hands desert me. It all began with the little finger of my left hand. The pianist on paper's fingers are numb. I expected to go blind. The Shadow attacks where you least expect it. Death nips at my hands. Might my hands kill me this summer? "One may very well die before death." One writes this sentence without trembling. Or perhaps with trembling. Perhaps it is more deeply more secretly true than one thinks. Shall we play? Still the heart feels tight under the T-shirt. I have survived my Isaac-death for ten years. Yet it nipped my throat, and dragged me out of the world.

There must be a good reason why, when one has left life behind, one returns, lifeless, to live on, at least for a while, as happened to Kriemhild, after she'd spent two days and two nights on the other side dead alongside the beloved cadaver. Without the bottomless need for vengeance to lift her from her grief, she would never have come back. Extreme suffering made her despair even of death. A violent need for vengeance is stronger than the need for rest.

It came to me yesterday that this entire book revolved around our Towers. I was in the mother house, in Arcachon, as if in New York. Cheek to cheek with Paradise. Thus very close to New York. In other words, very close to hell and its fires. Consequently, hoping for resurrection.

That's how it goes in my Providence.

Each time we resuscitate, the entire play resuscitates, Manhattan is also Oran, and then Osnabrück via Jerusalem, and the Arcachon bridge, all the places where fear began to lay siege to love, and the fire started

When I am in Manhattan, I am as close to Heaven as when I am writing in Arcachon.

When I am writing, everything is in the present. Time follows me.

It's not *I* who write, it is *my special providence,* Almighty Writing. She remembers me when I forget. She wakes me up before it's time, I haven't finished reading my dream when I hear her and all her birds singing, one after another, the whole chorus, right away I am ravished and convinced, I believe them, they guide me, no one will make me change my mind, I say yes to the thrush followed by the redbreast followed by the blue tit, I'm coming, I'm coming, wait for me. This is the moment when the dead are released, separation's truce, what a relief, and everyone is fine as usual, Mama, my father, the eternal beloved, my children, my animal incarnations; of course, our special dispensation is somewhat fragile but for the moment we shine forth, and Mama really is astir in her room. This is reality, what responds without fail to the birds' telephone. It is the same time it was an hour ago, to my right Hamlet and Horatio whisper, I know each word—they are Isaac's words. Not that he is their author. Montaigne too is murmuring at his window. Just lean towards the chink in the wall on the west side of his room and you'll hear them exhaled among the trees of the domain. And for each person each time it's the same mystery that nourishes the same thought: how not to forget to exercise one's freedom, how to cultivate the life after life. One can cross to death's far side: each person must rise to the challenge.

What I Find in Mama's Bottom Drawer

In the black dawn I enter my mother's belly. Nothing left here, I think. Empty room, vault I have eviscerated. To prevent the tomb's pillage I myself have pillaged it. Don't hope, nothing left here for the famished except the word "famished."

An hour drained of time spent in the dark, an hour of eternity without Mama.

It is a treasure-house, exhaustible and inexhaustible, Paradise in a chest of drawers, a world henceforth still alive sleeps in these four drawers. I have come to visit, explore, rummage Mama, just a little, before this Monday, this ordinary Monday, gets going.

Coo-coo! Coo-coo! To the west the cuckoo tunes up. Sol! Sol! La! La! The cuckoo is me. Sit down on her bed, on Eve's bed, Eve, merge with her body's invisible presence, impalpable and yet, with the body of her invisible presence, be Eve.

In the big white closet, her clothes breathe, and the sediments of her different periods, pretty white dresses some polka-dotted others striped all mythological. Here is a shoe box: Underpants! The big elegant letters traced in Eve's hand. Her need to document. To classify. Underpants. These garments are panties. Eve's panties, by metonymy: Eve. Her herbalist's soul. Panties remain.

From far off, from the bed, I see the drawers of the piece of furniture that I have, sadly, decided to empty almost completely, fearing that the tomb might be ransacked. What a pity! As if I'd gutted a chicken, a body, an enterprise that ruins in order to preserve. What I've left in the drawers, because they are of no obvious interest to a thief: *the recipes.* Eve's monument. Their value is in their number, I mean, their number-lessness. Shades of innumerable secret desires. So many of them! Exploration, held at bay, retreats. A great army. I'm going to count you, I think. But a kind of animistic fear keeps me from launching an attack on these myrmidons. Here is the untold invasion, a paper version of locusts. The awful feeling they are about to attack. They have a secret life, a mysterious malice. Touch one: you graze a beak. Hundreds of them, a conservative estimate. Here is a long life spent preserving hal-lucinations of food production, a colossal granary in a drawer. This is my mother's personal library. So she was a mental cook, a war chef. Here is the trace of a craving that no time no food no lover will ever satisfy. A whole faithless theology: she never made a single recipe. Day after day, year after year, she cooks the same meals à la Eve, plain, quickly assembled, spiceless, nothing fancy, modest, without trimmings, except for the colorful presentation of the starters, radishes, say, straight out of a child's drawing. Or were these recipes secrets confided, volup-tuous dream-letters, sublimated meals, drafts for amorous propositions, erotic thoughts addressed to the dream lover who never came, in whose place we had a succession of *Kümmerer,* caregivers with whom we made do.

So these recipes might hold the promise of Baudelairean beds; the drawer bulging with hundreds of alluring cards a vanity exuding per-fumes and incense. My mother never followed up on these invitations. Still, there is an *oeuvre,* I tell myself, a complete archeology of taste, the story of an ill-nourished German survivor of the 20s until 2013, ninety years at least on the trail of the senses. From now on, the mausoleum rests in peace, hidden from passersby.

The bottom drawer—I don't open. I spy on it. Three meters away, I perch on Eve's bed. We stare at each other, the drawer and I, we don't open. In the space between us night seeps away. We look at each other, eyes as still as two cats playing chess. Will renunciation win the day? Suddenly I stand up and march towards the drawer. I move at the tortoise-like speed of the mathematician Benjamin Fedorovich when he walks onto the first land-mined page of Mandelstam's *Fourth Prose*. "He tries to hold back the dangerous course of the disease." I go cautiously, which gives me the possibility of renouncing mid-crossing. I go hesitatingly. In the end, the tortoise always goes.

"Thatremindsme," says my mother's voice, which my insistent presence has conjured up, "of Gefühlte Kuchen, whose dough you had to leave overnight in the a pan under the quilt for it to rise, which generally did not work for my sister Eri, whereas for me it always did, as if the dough knew what it was doing, and because Eve rhymes with believe," my mother voice says.

—OK, I'm going, I say.

"Thatremindsme," says the voice, "of your way of going in reverse to Jerusalem, as if you didn't really want to, as if you were going where all flesh goes."

One goes the way of all flesh more and more slowly over time, it is time and space that thicken as the narrator's kiss flies towards Albertine's cheek, just before it crash lands

And I find:

Towering over the city, soaring and majestic as God's two legs, youthful, androgynous, and tender pink giants in the silence of the sky as if they celebrated the feast of beauty while down below on earth the microscopic city swarms: these are our Towers; they aspire to life's triumph.

"The closest
some of us
will ever get
to heaven"

Who said that? Who dared proclaim that some of us will never get closer to heaven? Surely not Emily Brontë? Or: This is the closest that any of us will ever get?

These two towers belong to whoever wants to scale them. Average daily population: 50,000 people work in the World Trade Center, and 80,000 visit every day. 130,000 people flow around us never doubting that the Towers are our history's columns. The more the people the more unique we are; and our secret gains in depth. The crowd rushes on and knows not what it hides in its flow.

Just board one of the seventy-two elevators to heaven, or as close as you can get. Alberich is the ferryman. A German from the Rhineland. He is a most energetic dwarf; he holds in his hand a stout gold whip. For Windows on the World, go straight to the 107th floor. You can't go any higher. There are 43,000 windows in the Towers. But these are special. They take your eyes straight to the eyes of Lady Liberty. And from there to the six windows from which Montaigne's Tower contemplates the universe. I have always felt the Semaphores watched over our travels. Many lovers whose eyes were full of friendship have led those who would become as dear to them as life itself to these sumptuous window-worlds. My mother and her sister had reserved a table for two at the Hors d'Oeuvrerie. Each time we pick and choose between The Cellar in the Sky, The City Lights Bar, or The Statue of Liberty Lounge, and every time we choose The Restaurant. Every time, we were as content as the first time. Guests were impeccably received. These Towers greet everyone alike.

These Towers are our towers, this no one can deny, we paid with our lives to enjoy them in perpetuity. My mother—her voice—says there's no such thing as *eternal*, but it's a word nothing in our language stops. The service is excellent, the prices fair, but she prefers the Empire State Building, where our cousin Richard Katz, like all the employees of the building's banks, has access to the staff canteen. We eat just as well lower down, my mother says, but Eri disagrees. I think Isaac always had in his heart of hearts a presentiment. But in the Restaurant we had windows on the world and I wasn't thinking about later.

The maître d'hôtel recommends the wild salmon, it is us he is advising, he is part of our history, his name therefore is Rumold the Nibelungen master-chef. It is to us he says:

The closest / some of us / will ever get / to heaven.

This is printed in capital letters on the menu.

—Perhaps not everybody wants to be that close to heaven, you say. But we voluntary reprobates have our entitlements. —The maître d' looks threatening, don't you think? you say. But the salmon is truly delicious, the summum of salmon, the man has not lied. If the menu sounds a warning, either we don't hear it or we aren't listening.

Death began here, on the Eternity floor, but we were oblivious. We didn't know we knew. *Eternal*, I say to my mother, exists as long as we don't know that we know.

By dint of thinking about dying we die. Some people, whom Montaigne quotes and imitates, think of it so assiduously that dying is all they do, over and over. In the end, the hour of death never comes because it is always already the guest at the table. But we were blissful dying

Up there, in God's lap, one is almost in Paradise. People have been able to pass the time there since April 1973. The Towers remember that they were once the two trees of the Garden of Eden. They are not buildings, they are expressions of our Nostalgia. When we were little, we were immortal.

And now, towards evening, the two boles are suddenly clothed in a golden light brushed on their bark by the setting sun, and today is so lovely that we have eyes only for this epiphany, we forget the anthill city, the job, the human condition; supernatural Nature reigns, and we fall prey to absurd desires such as Descartes himself had trouble resisting, like having "a body of a matter as incorruptible as diamonds." So we must heed the advice at the bottom of the World Trade Center's brochure, even if it is in small print as if the Authorities were reluctant to spoil the pleasure:

And in the evening, please don't touch the stars.

1611

1611, date of the first production of Isaac's *Tempest*

What were-we-doing-so-close-to-heaven? Almost. We almost. In reality, like all emigrants since the invention of these Islands on the shores of the year 1611 in order to take in the survivors of all the mythological shipwrecks, we have made land in a New World. We've pitched our camp in the forests of Broceliande, in 1971 we made love in a shaggy meadow on the banks of the Marne, at one o'clock in the morning in Latin we slipped through the chinks of Oxford's youthful walls, in 1993, guided by Ovid, we groped for each other in the dark but didn't die; I've waited for you, trembling, in the following lands: Canada, Spain, England, Portugal, Iceland, Japan, the USA, India, and I forget, but I've just this very moment realized that the injunction against touching the stars because they are fragile is the same in the Oxford night—while we tremble with desire—as in the night of the World Trade Center, O the name, the most beautiful in the world, how to resist it

—O the name! That force in the letters, able to cause a fatal swoon, each time I've obeyed it as I would a gibbering oracle

in 2000 as in 1940 we answer the same call, we return to the same source, every cell of our body receives creation's abiding message, we are summoned, we salmon, we are salmon ready for seven deaths to swim back to the point of origin we o bey without o bedience without knowing how everything repeats itself we heed the or der

all unawares we obey the letter we bear

I have always obeyed the letter O, obstinately I have made my way under the sign of O, as an ox to the ford at the address his fathers handed down, I was born to cross rivers, when I followed you to Oxford I didn't know that I was once more stepping into the Osnabrück ford, already I had already followed you in another life, I couldn't have done otherwise, before loving we love

Ox ford is Os nabrück in the other language

and the willows on the edge of the rectilinear water and the swans are the same

What were we doing up close to heaven? A truce. A few disaster-free hours between two wars, like the year that trembles between millenniums at Windows on the World, with its view of the present suspended, we are stowaways on the year 2000, always the clouds, the fear of being recognized and denounced that adds zest to the joy of the dying at not being dead, not yet; on the 107th floor of time we shelter briefly from time, homeless we are in The Restaurant, our luxurious Flying Saucer, we have paid for a peace served up by the maître d', of Burgundian or Egyptian origin, whose American name I forget,

The function of such characters is to see to their guests' pleasure while reminding them that death has designs on our felicity, but only when they bring the bill and not before

At times I was so close to heaven that I forgot to write, this was perhaps in 1978 or 1980. At such moments I didn't feel the need to write, I could walk on clouds without a balance pole. I had but one desire and this desire surpassing all desire was everywhere in me and all of me. Touch Isaac, not quite, barely; graze his hand with one finger for a second and—the ardent sensation of possessing God and not losing a crumb. The infinitesimal flutter of his eyelashes in my direction—a brazier. Each mouthful is his body on my tongue. We made love so violently with our eyes that we seemed to hear them crying out. Or our feet carried on a rapid conversation, laughing, under the pines, we remembered the garden's pomegranates in flower. —I am beyond death, and you? —Do what you have to do—I have a hundred hungers. For such delight I would give the second half of my life, the victory of creation, long summers at my papers. —How much time do we have? —Do you mean our lives? —I mean for lunch. (I laugh, he is wearing a straw-yellow shirt.) —Forty years still, will that do? —Watch over us because we are in danger. All the books say so. All the characters that we have been in one of our pasts came to a premature end. —We'll continue this discussion the next time we come. —Was everything satisfactory? the maître d' asks. Our accomplice is wearing his mummy suit. He's not sure when death is expecting us he says, but will give it some thought.

For now we are in no danger. On the 107th floor we drift on our deep time, from the origins, the source, the first thoughts. Once more our fête when? Both of the apocalypse moons are out. Happiness so sure, so frail. Thirty more years. And what if it's three? Or one?

I won't forget the year of the straw-yellow shirt. I was there.

Were it not for death's premeditation one could live without writing. But I had already had to die more than once, I write in anticipation.

What's most heart-wrenching about the 107th floor, Provisional Paradise, is that it is not impossible to go back. You leave it as you leave a mother, smiling, knowing she'll be there waiting for you. In my toilet bag I had the Open Sesame matchbox from Windows on the World, our amulet, that all-powerful bit of cardboard, frail memory in which we put our trust before the internet. I have it still. You wouldn't believe how indestructible my box is. I will carry it to the grave. It is our pocket tomb. His box, its twin, lives somewhere in the French National Library archives, I fear for it, it is so small, our mummy-in-miniature, and its pyramid is so big; I deposited it, it is more powerful than my fear, 2 centimeters by 5 centimeters are the dimensions of the world capsule. It contains eighteen nanotowers. One and a half million cubic meters of earth and rocks were excavated to make space for the vertical Bible of One World Trade Center. But nothing was lost. This noble matter was dumped into the Hudson River and turned into a vast stretch of Park.

Dust, before returning to Dust, in the meantime you have lifted the Book of Desires almost to immortality. Billions of Twin Towers brochures say so, and reading one from A to Z, in its febrile pages I am moved to discover a naive version of the Iliad and the Odyssey. Many modestly heroic human beings united to give form to their sense of pride. Twenty-five thousand artists haunted by a single image and ready to sacrifice themselves to bring it into the world.

I write:

    "The closest
    some of us
    will ever get
    to heaven"

—it seems to me there's a foot missing, my daughter says—where? I say; lost for a moment, I imagine God limping. In fact, I'm always afraid I'll lose the brochure, isn't it the witness, the sole survivor of the catastrophe? Viewed from the desk, it has the tall slender rectangular form of our Towers, a glossy sacred paper doll.

—it's 3, 3, 4, 3 feet my daughter says, knowledgeably attentive. *Some of us,* that's nice, it's anxiety-provoking this some of us, are we among the elect? One doesn't know whether the speaker is in or out, the speaker is one of *us,* but perhaps not part of the *some.*

Doubt was not us, at the time I had no doubt: we were among the few condemned to the promised proximity, I tell myself

(A sign of election: none enter here tieless. On that day, after a last-minute hesitation, you chose a tie with tigers rampant)

—this is the harsh secularization of a Christian thesis, my daughter says

Some seems *random,* one doesn't know how it happens that *some are in* and *some are out.*

What kind of chance selects those who are destined to touch heaven?

Strangely, the poem does the opposite of what it says, it begins with the closest, the further you read the farther away you get.

Ever, my daughter says, that conveys modality, it introduces a further element of doubt. The *ever* is what makes this line longer. Who knows how long *ever* may last?

And there you have it, the game of English accentuation makes the strongest beat of the entire poem fall on *ever.*

In my opinion, Donne gives himself over here to a parody of the logic of being saved. One hears the refrain of the straight and narrow.

—You, there! —No, not you! Them. —Us? Why us?

It is always frightening to be chosen. In order to live happy let's live hidden, says my mother's voice. Let's hide! Isaac says. Don't tell anyone. Don't touch the stars. For us, no such luck. The stars fell on us.

No one was there when the stars fell on us. What was done was done. The endless night of the present absolute reigned in the grotto. Creation itself had not yet been created. We had probably left our families, our professions, our shoes in the hall. Inside, in the absence all future attributes, there is neither memory nor law; an all-powerful Grace carries us one around the other, the only explanation is the force of attraction.

In the beginning is the response, a being's whole body responds to a being already with his whole body in a state of response even before answering the questionnaire. We are preceded, I say. Decided, Isaac says. Precipitated. Surpassed.

The closest, that's it.

The closest, a superlative of spatial nearness, pertains to a fantastic topology inherited from Christianity, my daughter says

—I am suspicious of superlatives, the voice of my mother says. — *The closest to heaven*, but not quite there, my daughter says. She scrutinizes the poem as one might scrutinize Leonardo da Vinci's drawing of a flying man flying.

—Thatremindsme of cousin Hans Jonas the twin who was a communist, at night he dreamed that he was an airplane pilot, after Auschwitz he really did become a colonel in the Air Force and mayor of Pankow. But Peter the twin who was not communist died in the camp anyway he was afraid of airplanes. There's a providence for all but where is the explanation, says my mother.

—It depends on the connotative charge of *Heaven* in the days of Donne, my daughter says. Souls go to *Heaven*. Bodies to the *Sky*.

—In German *Himmel* works for both, it's more practical, says my mother. My fear is that one day both sky and earth will be filled with the dead, we'll end up burying on the moon.

—What, for you, would the closest to heaven be?

All that is just advertising, says my mother. I haven't the least desire to eat that high up, it doesn't change the taste but it does change the price.

The Tooth

But during the meal while I'm savoring each morsel of Isaac, sucking the marrow of his every word, noting every eyelash flutter, an abrupt change

of intonation, I completely forget the cathedrals and their builders and the outstanding Event is the sudden loss of a tooth. Destiny strikes, Isaac gives a disgusted groan. Losing a tooth is these circumstances is not just losing a tooth, it's more, much more, clearly. Montaigne turns up with his lugubrious bill. One should always be booted and ready to go. What? What's wrong? Death—it's a part of you. In the midst of life we are in death, and viewed from the summit of the Tower, death is sweet, your tooth partakes of the world's life. Can I have it? I say. — You can't imagine how the area around my heart is sore, but never mind, says Isaac. It's as if a beast gnawed there.

Already in 1990, in the peak of health, when they had thirty years ahead of them according to their oracle, but the auguries were less rosy, *the fall of a sparrow*. There is a special providence in the fall of a sparrow.

—That's all a joke. *It is but foolery.*

As if there were a providence that confounded the auguries.

—It's not a tooth for a tooth. It's a tooth for you.

That said, you look at me with your mouth shut, smile transferred to the corners of your eyes while I slip the tooth into the matchbox, where it lives today as thirty years ago, in my toilet bag. What a trip!

—When you look at the portrait of the Towers you see wraiths. Those who ascend the Towers from within never see these creatures of the imagination. Crystal mountains incarcerated in the City's gullet. The scene represents the artist's secret thoughts, it respires the solitary pride of the work. Not a sign of life. They are Ideas. Above the imperceptibly madding crowd, the columns stand apart from the earth as if they sought to take root in the sky, but which sky? Spiritual vessels whose beauty no puny human can see unless he hires a plane. Made for the enchantment of gods and birds, here are the Towers as you will never see them. That there should be two of them goes back to Genesis. In my opinion, the artist, like God, sought to spare his creature the torment of solitude. Says Isaac. Who orders an infusion. Verbena. Because of the word. In French. *Verveine.*

—Tell me a memory, I say.

—Off the top of my head?

—Yes, the first person to reach the 107th floor of the World Trade Center.

And, as when Ulysses invoked the land of the dead, I see the ghosts troop up, but little Elpenor pushes ahead of them all. I really wasn't expecting his anxious small self, so many are the memories worth celebrating.

I don't recall the dining room's paneling and the two-century-old heir-loom silverware stamped with the initials of this Saint John. I do remember some of the obstacles that nourish desire, don't turn the lights on, let silence clothe the night around the inflamed heads, like a wall of bricks

ex aequo captis ardebant mentibus ambo, as if the wall had a small chink, setting both of them ex aequo afire with passion, me coming at midnight from one side, you on the other, and lip to lip our warm breath touched, and each in haste planting kisses or sighs on their side of the partition

—In the end I unlocked the porch. In your fake-student hood, you look like a fake monk

—See what you make me do? In silence in the stairway and in the antique high bed under the quilt as in a fairy tale, don't turn the light on, never as dark outside as within splendor, our fingers touched the stars, don't cry out, I won't

were we rehearsing Pyramus and Thisbe in *A Midsummer Night* or Ovid's tragedy? Hardly had I touched the thick wall, *Invide, dicebant, paries, quid amantibus, obstas*? Wall, don't come between us, we are not ungrateful: we know we owe you this chink through which our words go straight to the beloved ears, don't cry out, they'll hear us, and in the ancient staircase off he goes

—What's wrong with me, Doctor? —That? It's herpes. —Herpes? But how? How?

—By contamination. By a fairy tale. I hear Satan chortle: serves you right. A tale of transmission. —But I only made love with my lover *my only love.* —It can sleep for a long time, a long time. —For twenty years? Dormant? 'Transmission, transmission,' the title of one of his poems. —Him, only. Only him. So him not only?

Don't think about it. A ghost story. One is haunted. Don't think about it. *Thus it will make us mad.* Do you remember the Night of Saint John? The stars under the sheets.

No I cannot write that. Write it! Do the thing you cannot do.

Let us return to the Restaurant, where he has finished his verbena.

—In the throng of the dead, Elpenor is the one who comes back? Let us bury him, as he begged us to.

—Let's not get all worked up in front of this innocent brochure.

—I should have taken one of those brochures, I think as we leave the Tower, but I'll get one the next time.

—When will we come back, they wonder, will we come back? Do you think we'll come back?

We'll come back in 2001, I say, 2004 at the latest, we say, we'll come back next year, they say, in the taxi they've taken for Brooklyn, they recite the numbers that gleam like pearls on time's necklace. Later, hearing the crystalline sound of those dates they were to feel a tremendous pain.

Never had we been so alone. Alone in the solitude that the wonder of happiness secretes. Alone like those two swimmers in the Ocean at seven o'clock on the dawn of the year 2000; from far away one can't discern the characteristics of the coming century and millennium, only the sparkle of their rose-tinted gold dust. How lovely the times ahead of us would be. For the moment we know nobody here and nobody knows us, we are still as much strangers as if Shakespeare had not existed, we resemble no one, we have no names

Meanwhile my mother is lunching with Eri and Richard Katz in the Empire State Building's employee canteen, but I don't know this yet

I didn't take a brochure away with me. This one was taken by my mother. She didn't know that by tucking this slip of paper into her backpack she was acting according to the magical thinking attributed to her by our destiny: a role of absolute fidelity guided blindly by love. At every turn she responded unawares to my extravagantly vital needs, moved by ultraconscious data communicated by invisible waves. —You need green beans? Spinach? —I've got that too. These market offerings translated into color the spiritual provisions she never failed to supply me. Besides, the images on the folder are a spinachy-cauliflower color. If she'd known, she wouldn't have done it. How could we have known?

Could "German romanticism" have prompted her firmly anti-romantic spirit? On occasion she would come right out and admit to finding in herself some ridiculous residual trace of it.

While I was in New York on life's frontiers with Isaac, she was in New York with Eri. From afar as from close up, Eve watches over me as a goddess watches over her tender and vulnerable hero.

How could we have known that concerning our life *as close as one can get to Heaven* only a slender brochure stored in my mother's bottom drawer would remain, in case I should be flung like flotsam onto one of time's deserted quais?

The Bottom Drawer contains a certain number of synonyms for my mother's soul. These pink cliffs of Zion, which have journeyed from Palestine to Utah, this Garden of the Gods in Colorado Springs, this Balanced Rock teetering on the tip of its nose, these granite monoliths in Yosemite, these are the forces of her nature, her innocent grandeurs. Eve wanders in the midst of these unshakeable phenomena like the Paiute Indians who feel that they belong to Zion, not that Zion belongs to them.

According to her, the Towers are a vulnerable imitation of Nature's Temples. She prefers the Empire State Building. Something in the energy of its constructor recalls her father, the Strasbourg factory builder, the enterprising merchant who invented the concept of the industrial suburb, according to my mother. Clinging with Eri to the Observatory balustrade, my mother felt "the spirit" of Michael Klein "speak" to her of his dream of Empire in America. But she dismissed this moment of ghostly communication as just the kind of "bunkum" her daughter is capable of coming up with. That's the wind, not her father's spirit

—You read your books I need you sitting beside me. I've no idea what you're running on about, says the voice of my mother. That's literature. You're talking about our trip to New York in 2000. What happened?

We await the explanation. And in the end no explanation. I'll tell you what happened

The Empire State Building

Eri and I, we didn't have to pay to get into the Empire State Building because our cousin Richard Katz invited us. Now he's retired but he still has the right to the staff canteen. The husband of Hilde who was already dead, otherwise we'd have had lunch with her. He was a teller at one of the banks.

That Eri she has some nerve, whereas me I was embarrassed. And what did she order? A Pork Chop! I nearly fell off my stool. Wouldn't you know, with the cousin who is Orthodox she has never eaten pork, and all of sudden, I don't know if the Empire State went to her head, and Richard Katz stuck his nose in his plate and didn't say a thing. That Eri is really thoughtless. He is our host. He trusts us. To begin with, he's our cousin. And two, we're his guests. Next, there's no reason *whatsoever* to order a pork chop, it's totally uncalled for. It's as if Eri stuck a knife in the Empire State Building. I compare it to a fantasy attack. That's how you get yourself noticed

And you, what did you eat, up there in your clouds?

And there you have it, how the Empire State Building enters the legend, thanks to Eri's famous chop. Something about these Towers gives the souls of dreamers a reckless urge to transgress

Hilde was also the daughter of Aunt Paula, third of the three Jonas sisters, the one who used to put her piece of cake on top of the armoire so no one could touch it or maybe not, maybe that's Selma who used to count peas. She married her cousin and they didn't go to South Africa, they managed to get to the USA

My mother conjures up the whole Osnabrück history across Oran across the generations, goes to New York, from restaurant to subway, pauses for a peek at Madagascar, she won't go there, it's too late, her one regret is Easter Island, this time it was Hans Gunther not Eri who missed the plane. The other times they missed the plane it was because Eri can never leave on time, she always has to leave at the last minute

In the course of the voyages, you also voyage by evoking all the voyages, you no longer know in which voyage you are being voyaged, when Mister Ulysses dines with his son in Ithaca he is in Knossos Ithaca New York, things grow complicated, how you get from dining in Paris to dining in New York where at the age of seventy Eve and Eri come and go from the Gramercy Hotel to Queens on the subway, from Cousin Fred or someone else, a cousin yet another one, Gerta's children, the word cousin on every side, the book's job is to take charge of the muddle

The little cousin says: *jetz wollen wir ruddeln*. Do you know this word? Eve asks. *Ruddeln?* Yes, I say. *Ruddeln* is Gerta's daughter's word, her motto her heritage; because of *Ruddeln,* the secret name of secrets, Eve meets Gerta's daughter; I have never heard it spoken, except in the book that Eve doles out to me, little by little, fragments of chapters torn from the chaos following the collapse of the Jonas family Tower

After the war, I say, they adopted the boy and left the girl in the orphanage? Is that the subject of the *Ruddeln*?

But Eve doesn't answer. By definition, *Ruddeln* always happens under a cloth of silence. It's a matter of tell-don't-tell something, to whisper a secret, to hidesecrete it, swaddle it in mute paper, abolish it, bake it to ash and cinders, nudge it off to the side and forget it. The thing is done. Hush it. Crush it. Secrete it. What's done is done. This is the triumph of exsecretion: the very word ssssht has been carried away in yesteryear's snow no one knows when, no living person knows of it now. It doesn't exist. A handful of the dead, who'd read Rabbi Bacharach's grimoire once knew it. It is the women who *ruddeln*

I myself don't know this word. I say: Yes, I recognize it. But what does *ruddeln* mean? It comes to crush everything underfoot and turn it to mush

each and every time the sad scene of sorcery is re-enacted in New York. In this scene, Gerta's daughter goes to court against the family crime, an interminable mixed-up crime, unrepaired re-begun protected and disavowed by every witness, and no god and no tragic author has taken her side. In this scene, my mother is the chorus. The daughter shouts murder; the rescued son shuts up, my mother is embarrassed, she thinks that if Hilde couldn't adopt both of her assassinated sister's children nobody knows why she chose the son and left the daughter behind. Of this, no one has ever spoken.

In the end, she, my mother stops, baffled, and says: it's complicated.
Let's stick with *Ruddeln*.

—That's what family is.

What good are the memories? says my mother. What good being
born at Recklinghausen? Or in Essen. Since you won't be able to come
back. Now I am mixing up Hans and Peter. Do I know whether my
grandfather was born in Borken? —In Gemen, says Eri. —Why bother
fighting over a birthplace? The main thing is to know where you are
going to die.

Where shall we meet again? During my life, I was a leather merchant
in Paraguay. In the end, we'll all meet up at the Empire State Building.

—Where are you going? asks the porter, yet another former
German. —We have an appointment with Richard Katz. —*Which one?*
So there is more than one. The one on the 66th floor. *There are seven
Richard Katzes in the building.* Richard Katz 66.

Seven, just in this building, it gives you pause. Richard Katz was much
appreciated by his superiors. An honest accountant. It proves one can
survive anything and multiply. One of the Richard Katzes, the one on
the last floor, do you know him? The architect? —We didn't know there
was an architect in the family. —What one could have been. I wanted
to be a doctor, says Richard Katz 66. —In the end a bailiff. Not to be.
To become.

It is as if the Empire State Building were a colossal metamorphosis
of the Bible, the great book of the nomadic exiles. —So it's the
Promised Land? —No. Here, it's Ecclesiastes.

Richard calls Eri 'Rosi,' no one knows whether this is inadvertent or out of confusion. Rosi is Eve and Eri's mother's name. Epochs touch. Eri is vexed. But in the Building of Time isn't everything vanity? For my mother, one cousin is as good as another. And one floor as good as another. The main thing is to be useful.

Ruddeln, no one knows that in Germany any more. It has disappeared.

Once upon a time, the word *Ruddeln* lived in literature, it was in *The Rabbi of Bacharach.* In this tale, they hide a dead child under the Passover table. The little cadaver found on the priestly manure heap. For once in his life, he will have been good for something.

The tale lives on, hidden in the three volumes of the works of Heine, which have never left Eve's shelf. I have never read it. I don't know why. It has remained hidden like a dead child under the tablecloth.

Over time my mother's stories grow increasingly colorful and muddled. I notice that forgetfulness does not efface but heightens the surface of the subject, especially with the color red. The Bacharach tablecloth seems to me scarlet. Its brightness hypnotizes me. Consequently, I don't look under the surface.

From New York the mind of my mother's heads back to Osnabrück.

(With a quick detour via Ascension where she met Fred, a cousin, or another.)

Perhaps it's here, on Fifth at Thirty-Fourth, that the Osnabrück-and-back Odyssey ends. In the next sentence, here we are on the corner of Nikolaïort.

I say: Act I the past—Act IV the present.

Eve says: there is none. (At that moment she was a hundred years old.)

Ruddeln! Perhaps that is this book's wish, and that of many an other as well: the pleasure to gossip and whisper, and with incomprehensive and deceiving words and without knowing what one does, write down that which must not be said; with *ruddeln* one can even speak ill and betray without fear, since everything is protected by a foreign language. Hence, there is pleasure in the moaning and groaning, not only in the pain. When everything stays in the family, like Eve and Eri in the Empire State Building-employee restaurant, one can truly speak a little ill of everyone.

This is what happens when a violent storm has shattered a family and scattered its genealogical seeds to the planetary winds. The spores of the Jonas mushroom have spread according to the principle of the ubiquitous theology. All around the world spring up lives and deaths full of fantasy.

A Pork Chop! Having succeeded in leaving Osnabrück for Paris in order to make it to Palestine in 1936 in order to swap Haifa for Cologne in 1950 and from Cologne take up most pleasant quarters in Manchester with all the kosher food you want at Marks and Spencer, you had to come to Manhattan to choose a Pork Chop?

—Is this how it worked in your family? the Jonas of Thirty-Fourth Street asks irritably. Typisch Klein! How very Kleinish! *Das hat er mir gesagt*, grumbles Eri the liberated woman.

Many wars and grudges that have poisoned families commence with the story of a pig or an apple.

Just like you and Granny Cixous says my mother, your cockeyed inventions were a blot on my reputation as a daughter-in-law.

In 1948, I began to feel the temptation of the comic, my father dead the world seemed to me a vast canvas of comedies, my imagination and I hiding under the gorgeous white sheets of classical antiquity; in beds deep as the caverns of my paternal grandmother I caressed my projects to write some Ididn'tknowwhat of which I hadn't the least idea, I had passions but no objects, I was wild about liberty, but being free I had trouble satisfying my penchant, I saw noble and grotesque, grandiosity lurked, with a father laid low in the glory of his youth, I preferred the beard on my Aunt Deborah's chin, a singularity that was at least as noteworthy as the black pimples on the tip of the nose of the Abbess of the Propagation, my grandmother was in all things Spanish, in austerities, in sobrieties, in black robes of mourning in mourning, and also in supernatural explosions of grief in the places assigned to sacrifice, if not my father's surgery then his tomb. There, on the little stage of pink granite, the unnamable trance starts. First my grandmother utters three explosive cries, so powerful you hear them on top of the mountain. It is as if her boiling heart vomited its breath into a shofar.

Then, from my grandmother, legs straddling the body of my father who is once more her son and only her son, like a giant divinity urinating on the world, comes a cow oozing blood, bright red, a young red, a velar maculation, a beast that bellows from the depths of the uterus the abduction of her calf, they slaughter it, the calf convulsed, she agonizes in her agony, the slaughterhouse is in her entrails, she will struggle until the flesh is stripped from the bones, a cry for a cut, all the blood in the world will not extinguish this cry

no one can stop the hemorrhage

useless to protect my ear drums, no cushion is thick enough to muffle the howls of tortured love

you'd think the cow were howling blood from every orifice, the assassination is long the pain inexhaustible

we all die in my grandmother's desperate avidity, the calf she fights the butcher gods for is not a father, is not a spouse, is not a brother, it is the fruit of her entrails, let no one contest that

If there is anybody in the world who pretends to die more than her, if there is anyone who can open wide to vomit more blood, if there is anyone who can liquefy themselves in flows of urine and excrements, if anyone can defy the inhuman mystery of the mother, if anyone can bray to split the clouds

seated behind the tomb, I try to eat my father but my imagination balks, I open my mouth wide, and what comes out? Great hiccoughs of laughter. That's how it happened.

In the cemetery, my grandmother is in rut, she wants an orgasm, she moans, her leaden feet crush my bones, she gives birth to her grief and licks the cadaver of the calf she didn't save, her nostrils drool mucus, sagging with age her two breasts hurt and that feels good, she has big strong laborer hands, her clamor causes the tiny brood that trails after her to tremble and shake and she doesn't give a shit, even an ass under the blows of a cudgel in its atrocious despair could not bellow so superbly

and me, hoarse, devoid of courage and recourse, I drop like a little stone far from the heights where the dead await us with outstretched hands.

I didn't know I didn't know how to cry. When my grandmother dug up her son and caressed my father's shining heart, I recoiled. Writing strode right past me and I didn't recognize it. My grandmother rears up and demands her stolen son back, how long the revolt will last no one can predict, is there a door at which to knock, for how long is it going to continue, this tragedy?

I devour an apple flesh core and pips I dream of a year with no month of February, no clots of tears no shattering sobs no dead calf no beast dripping myrrhs of maledictions

I crawl behind the tombs, I allow syrups of salted laughter to pour out, my fingers are purple with ink my hand is too clumsy to paint the end of the world I can't bray my lungs are too dry can't moan can't groan can't even bark my belly lacks entrails instead of writing I squeak I dread the grandeur of February the writing strides by and I don't hear it my ears are buried

The Bed is so big you could fall asleep there with the dog the cats and the rabbits, my cousin and I live in it, the vast whiteness of my grandmother's white sheets has the gift of inspiring me. I love slipping into them with my feet muddied by the day's history, this was when we used to go barefoot. Or is it that I like to kindle and I fear the anger of my grandmother whose cult of cleanliness I offend again and again. The Bed was all Oran *the closest we will ever get to heaven.* You couldn't not want to defy it. O purity! I experienced the clean. I defended the soiled.

The voice of my grandmother is like God's voice in the Garden of the Book of Genesis, it trots around yapping at the heels of the disobedient. A loud, rumbling voice like a laborer's hand. —Is this what your mother taught you? To blow your nose on the sheets?

The voice finds me under the sheet.

And I answer: Yes. At home we do that. We blow our noses on the sheets.

And my grandmother believes it.

And my mother says: Why did you have to say that?

However far from Oran she might be, sooner or later the news catches up with her.

My grandmother is Spanish to death. Let my mother receive a lover in her bed, it's none of her business, she shuffles past the bedroom door in her babouches and mum's the word. But blow your nose on the Bed's vast sheets and right away she makes it her business.

My mother does not understand why I would tell an untruth that gives birth to resentments and hostilities in the family. All it takes is one instance of a nose to stir up a Spanish side and a German side.

Europe's backbone bristles. Fifty years later, they'll still be bitter. The irritation began and I'm responsible, but in my view my grandmother started it. But, says my mother, it's me who pays.

Before the arrival of my German family in Oran, they'd never seen Ashkenazim, they didn't even know there was such a thing. And the Ashkenazim didn't know the Sephardim.

—What's the point? my mother says. I call that a gratuitous lie and a very costly one.

In my view, saying that at home we blow our noses on the sheets is not lying. In my view, the Bible is where it all began. There was a fault. And the history of writing began. It all started with a trial. To the question: who started? I respond: on the one hand my mother, on the other my grandmother, where is the truth? The truth is in the where, between the beds, between the mothers. You are doing what you must not do, says The Voice that pretends to be out for a stroll, and I tell the truth: yes, I am doing what I must do to launch the story: you must do what you must not do.

I side with the women who blow their noses on a fine mess of sheets.

Why did you say that? —So that my father's mother believed me. So she wouldn't believe me. To rub the truth with the garlic of the false. To add another layer. To add insult to injury. To exaggerate the sin by extolling it. To defend my mother by accusing her. To affirm the alliance between my mother and me. To proclaim the freedom to transgress. To have fun at my grandmother's expense. To practice the art of repartee. To soil. To defy the rules. To deserve the reproaches.

I play in the garden of the Bed, my grandmother is one of the play's tall marionettes, I lift the sheets and I exercise my right to invent reality.

My grandmother is a tower. A cliff that sways on its base. She is double. She is a twin tower, a creature with double locks.

What does the person who defends the cleanliness of her own Bed know about the person who bellows and shits in Cimmeria? And vice versa? We are possessed.

Who taught you to blow your nose on the tomb?

What is troubling is that the two worlds follow each other like day follows night without talking without ever acknowledging the other. After the crisis one leaves the other comes back, there is no answer. When she is in the land of the dead, my grandmother is someone else.

You never know about Eri, says my mother, if she's the one whose pork chop caused the Empire State Building and the entire Osnabrück archive to quake on their foundations—she's as full of surprises as one of Wilhelm Busch's good-for-nothings.

We Lie

Did Isaac know Comedy was the playbill at the Empire State while Tragedy and Epic played the World Trade Center?

He didn't.

He doesn't know that during this time my mother and her sister are sub rosa on Fifth Avenue. Or perhaps he does?

We lie, we do everything in the world to keep love safe, we hide, we dissimulate, we do not name our fears and dangers, we keep the secrets secret, lock one secret up under another, I never say we are on the fourth floor of the secret by my mother, we say nothing, when Isaac comes, I tell my mother: Go, and my mother goes, how would I survive without my mother's help without her silence without her absence, without the constancy of her indifference, without the keys to her apartment, does Isaac know this? I don't know. I don't know what he knows and doesn't know. Who cares that we didn't know what we don't know, love needs to be threatened and saved if it's going to survive. So, let's lie.

I tell her everything

I have to tell my mother: don't come, don't enter, don't put your keys in my lock, if you call I won't answer, we are naked, our two bodies painted on the bed, I look at the drawing of the double body that sleeps, you'd think it was a gold star in the sea of green salt, go see your cousin

I am able to speak to my mother without fear: love and so forth—for her is a foreign language, cactus, desert, it's nothing. How she knows how to keep things to herself I don't know the secret, she knows how not to know, to know for Eve means not to have, in the end I don't tell her anything

It's not lying when you lie to save your life, with the Jews you can even eat pig, says Mama, do it and don't tell, Saturday I went to see my cousin at the Rothschild Foundation, my cousin the hot water she didn't know if she could use it, fortunately the rabbi was there, and do you know what the rabbi said?—I am going to give it some thought. I was there when he said that. Ham, sometimes I eat it, you don't think I'm going to tell him?

Don't say anything, live

As for what he owes my mother, Isaac is in the dark really. What he knows he knows with the sort of magical, merciful not-knowing that breezes about the Towers

Up there in the Towers one knows nothing, one trembles, one prays, one laughs, one dares to despair of despair, and none of that can happen without Magic's unfailing help.

The great lovers lie body and soul. Say you are my sister, Abraham says, and underneath a silken fib Sarah goes along with him. The lie is the magic cloak that renders us invisible and serves as a visa to our evasions, Tristan says

Say that you are my sister, my love my sister, and let us weave a story in which to dress our story, in which we will be immortal, under the tent death will not shadow us, let us be the unchecked artists of waiting, let's write this Book that does not know the end, nor the date and whose duration is the miracle of the eternal today, let's be the authors of our fatalities, when I am dead continue, say you are my sister, dead I will live, death will not keep me from finding you as always. Nothing has changed, except for the telephone. I will invent another. Where will we meet? At my mother's as always, under the maternal tent. —What does your mother know? —My mother knows nothing.

I am not lying. What my mother knows, she could well not know. She knows how to know without knowing, that is her magic. Without her magic we could never have lived until now without losing our lives. Isaac prefers not to know what he knows, but he prefers not to know it, period.

Our tent is a mental fabrication, in appearance so fragile it would make a tortoise laugh. Still, it has turned out to be as solid in all weathers as a tortoise's carapace. My mother would sing German songs to the tortoise. I cannot say we had a tortoise. I would have loved to have one. But it was. My mother was singing. The tortoise listened or didn't. What is certain is that it went away. Inexorably. Where did it go? To its life. I was sorry for my tortoise. —Do you remember the tortoise? —No, I am too old. It went away. What on earth are you talking about? my mother says. —It happened in the Book, I say. —Another of your incongruities, says my mother. Thatremindsme of the pork chop. —Was it in the book or in reality?

When we lie, we are on love's straight path, and straight is good, we don't lie, we pull out all the stops, we write the Book with the stuff of our pain, we burn up, we reduce ourselves to ash, my ash is the subtle matter of my ink, when you write, under your fingers you make my blood flow with yours, you can write everything, whatever you create with my ash in touch with the paper becomes true. Don't forget that I am a forest, the paper says. I was dead and I come alive at your call.

Were Isaac and I really at *Windows on the World*, on Heaven's Balcony, while my mother and her sister were in the Empire State Building, in which reality, in which story, in which year? It was in the year 2000. In this book. In this book's reality.

You Never Know Who to Expect

My books are nautical self-constructions, I tell my daughter; free in their movements and in their choice of routes, they can take to air or water, founder or fly, be composed of several stories, jokes, eye-witness accounts, true or false. They are enriched with alluvial deposits from all the worlds, dropped into this or that chapter. A gracious contribution from the gods. They are the product of many makers, dreamed, dictated, cobbled together, augmented with fantasies, whence the plurality of their birthplaces. If, to take notes on the voyage, I am at anchor in my Aquitaine study, my spirits come and go among the Cities and times that inhabit the different floors of my mental library.

The readiness is all. Whatever the hour, the page, the rule of hospitality is what directs the Book. You never know who to expect, I tell my daughter. What the weather is like. How old you are. For which country you have a ticket. With whom you are about to quarrel. Today I encountered an ancient tortoise I hadn't seen since Algiers. She went away. Her going left me with a small ache of fatality. That she should depart was written. In spite of myself I was forced to love her. Because she loves music. Because the tortoise folk were in the garden a long time before the human colonization. Because you'll never hear her sob and wail.

Must the Book adopt her? —Did she leave a long time ago? my daughter asks.

—Sixty years. Nothing could have kept her. That's why I've never forgotten her.

—Tortoise rhymes with stubbornness, my mother says.

—I'm a little worried I say to my daughter. —Because of the tortoise? —Isn't it incongruous? —She's part of the family, my daughter says. —Do we lead destiny or does destiny lead us? Uncertainty is the soul of literature. —The fear of being incongruous is what's incongruous, my daughter says.

I seem to recall having been jealous of the tortoise. Because of her age. Because she carries time on her back.

There you had someone who listened to no one. She followed her being.

—I had a friend who used to say: *Ich bin so unanständig*: I am so indiscreet! my mother says. —Who was she? —I forget if it was Frau Engers or me, says my mother.

And we laugh.

Even in 1930 she was headstrong. She was a modiste. She was modest. She made hats too beautiful to be believed. She gave my mother her husband on a Friday. In 1925, perhaps.

Do we know where we are going? the Book asks. And you, where are you going? I remember Jacques, the Book says. The fatalist. A genuine hare-tortoise. A book that went very fast very slowly. Imagine a tortoise galloping. Jacques followed his master as you follow yours and his master followed his master as Jacques followed him. But who was the master's master?

I follow Jacques as I follow my mother. I would follow Isaac as if he were my mother. When Isaac went away, the tortoise came back.

My mother is a tortoise. Everything about her is tortoise-like: the slowness, the longevity, the neck, the indestructibility. Isaac sleeps. He's hibernating under the paper. I go out with my mother. We take tiny steps against the wind. My soul folds under a gust of grief. Jacques weeps without constraint for his captain who dies on page 95 and is resurrected on page 98. In the gust of wind I become teary. During the whole of our walk, my mother tells me about Pauline her hostess's niece. The next day: Today I'll tell you about the nephew, my mother says. And so we come to the small observatory. I say: Starting now, you stop. What do I have to do with nephews? My mother bursts out laughing and goes on talking. She says "the things of the past." I listen with the ear of the future that will be bereft the day the sempiternal "things of the past" no longer turn up.

I should have asked her what she was doing in the 15th arrondissement of Paris in the summer of 1942 instead of being in Oran sewing her couture robes, but that's a question no one can answer anymore; and how she managed to escape from the cordoned-off district, which would have interested me, but without Pauline I would never have been born. Without Pauline from Oran the young Eve from Osnabrück would never have met Doctor Georges Cixous; in 1935, she didn't yet have a chic-ish studio in the 15th.

This morning it is the year 2017, the 16th of July. When I wanted to get out of the house, to continue my memory walk, I couldn't open the gate. We are captives. It is written up there, the Book told me. By dint of following Jacques-who-follows-his-master-as-you-follow-yours, we find ourselves in prison like Aesop. Do I need to refresh your memory? "Like me, Aesop heads for the beach this morning. The police stop him: Where are you going? —Where am I going? I say, says the Book, says Aesop. I have no idea. —You have no idea?! Off to jail with you. Surely you know that you must know? What sort of book doesn't know where it's going? —Alright, says Aesop, didn't I just say I didn't know where I was going? I wanted to go for a swim, and now here I am in prison."

I have just finished reading what the Book tells me, I arrive at the gate. The lock is stuck. In my dreams, I'm always looking for a way out, a taxi, my car, my plane ticket for New York, the toilets, Isaac's phone number, Isaac's exit door, the tortoise's, I want to run, the road is barred,

but here, this is happening *in reality* like in a dream, reality itself has metamorphosed into an anxiety dream, into a prison, it's awful! reality is a prison, I was standing, beach bag in hand, everything came to a halt, unable to exit reality and without warning, a moment ago I was free, suddenly I'm stopped, a hopeless Sunday, I felt Adam and Eve's dread on the day and hour the story began, suddenly the gate is barred, I didn't think of the *Metamorphoses*, that's a fable, I was banished into myself in reality, no one around, the gate is so high, so hostile, the very picture of irony and cruel indifference, it's July 16, Pauline is rounded up on the Rue du Docteur Finlay, my mother's best friend. No Pauline.

I didn't think about it. I was petrified. I was up to my neck in anxiety, up to my brain. Trapped. Oh! I can understand the tortoise's flight. Later, I'll ponder the state of soul of the freed tortoise. The most humble and archaic of the Prometheuses. Right now later is far away and faceless. I note that from the very first moment of being shut up, time coagulates in my mind; instead of flowing, the minutes harden into a chaotic wall, they construct a Dantesque dam against thought. Maybe you can't see it but I'm walled in. I gasp through a chink borrowed from Pyramus and Thisbe.

My house is isolated. All writing houses are intentionally isolated. One spring day you retire there for good. After a death. You write a contract letter to yourself: the testament of birth. You speak of an "I" who is a You. You take yourself as witness. Today you are thirty-eight years old, you bear witness to dedicating yourself *istas sedes et dulces latebras avitasque libertati suae tranquillitatique et otio* to your freedom your peace and quiet and your leisure. You go into hiding. I began hiding at the age of twenty-three. It's the first time that the seat of my freedom has been transformed into a rabbit hutch

I have always feared prison, perhaps I have not always avoided it, according to my mother the vault preys on me, at night shaking with fear she comes: I can't sleep for worrying, the vultures sit there and you feed them, what's this kollok you're gibbering about? —It's about Derrida and me. —But Derrida is a philosopher, going to kolloks is bad for you, they bury you alive, all these people who exploit you, who cooks for you? That's why I brought up the croissants. —What croissants? I say. —The midwife who used to bring me croissants, she wanted a job at the Clinic. In a twinkling I said: Out! No corruption! These kolloks are poisoned croissants. Be reasonable, listen to your mother, it's not because he's a philosopher you have to give them something palpable, a whole life's work you want to hand it to them? Don't fatigue people, they aren't philosophers, get out of your cage, get down to the level of ordinary people, quit overdoing it, why bother, no one listens, you don't help anyone. It's like your friend the poet, you think a poem is worth suffering over? Proust! You think he had a good life? A kollok on Proust? I say: Forget it! Your mother is a sage but nobody listens to her message

In the blink of an eye the garden has turned into a citadel, the hedges palisades, I should never have locked the gate, I should have listened to Montaigne, I armed my house instead of trusting its safekeeping to heaven. All the buried-alive I know of have surrounded me, I had always read *A Premature Burial* as Poeian exaggeration and now here I was walling myself in

And without the help of Marcel, the Book and I might have perished in the labyrinth.

Every cloud has a silver lining, says Jacques. The Fatalist. Without the gate disaster I'd never have managed to slip Marcel into the book. It was about time. Marcel is the living pillar of everything I write. I cannot imagine concluding my life without signaling my gratitude. No place to rest, no temple, no book; no tower, no Essays, no place to call home, no bookshop, no anonymous maternal figures, no cathedral; I know the name of the little man who bears the cathedral of Rouen on his back and with whom the cathedral shares the secret of immortality, the little man in whom Ruskin recognizes the most modest technician of the work of art, the representative of hardworking humanity, the direct descendent of the historical Adam, the Adam who set to work.

Marcel freed me. He came like the Messiah. He came from the next town. I was shouting: I can't get out! And the voice of the old woodsman scarred by his battles with the elements responded: I'm coming! Here I am! And three hours later he clambered over the wall on a tall ladder. "For as long as I still can," he says. He's the handyman of last resort. The divine sculptor made him with big hands, of a beauty that Time cannot attack, the hands of genius, in his image. Stronger than anything. My hand is small and quick as a squirrel, and weak and fearful in equal measure. My hand leaps unhesitatingly and anxiously. Perches a moment like a wren on the broad back of Marcel's Hand, and flits off. For fifty years the tranquility of my writing hand has been kept safe by Marcel's big vigilant hands. "I support you," his hand says. My hand trips off, where it goes, what it does, the guardian hands know no more than I do. "Off you go."

As for me, "I won't budge," Marcel thinks, no need for a speech.

My true freedom, my principal retreat and solitude are so well founded on Marcel that if I didn't have an ever-on-the-alert squirrel heart, I could settle into my human tree right to the outskirts of oblivion.

We can't do everything. Very often my books have been protected by demi-gods from the mythological regions of my life.

Marcel is consubstantial with my writing house. You will find him nowhere else. Like the forest men who once were trees, he will never leave his land. A root does not go jaunting about.

Today the Towers are trees without roots, Isaac says, one cannot imagine such unstable colossi. When we alight on them in on our annual migration I'm always afraid that they will have been carried away by a storm. But they are still here, a powerfully fragile miracle. We have no earthly roots either. We are bound to each other by memory and repetition. By dint of secretly returning to New York and then rising to the 107th floor, we grow a strange mental garden where we stroll for a few days, as in eternity before the Fall, two growing trees whose roots reach for the sky, one time we were there for Rosh Hashanah. "Today," Isaac writes, "I see them as pyramids that will shelter us and live on without ever having been aware of anything."

One day he sees them dead. One day he sees us dead, they live on and see us dead

Since our celebration at the Tower, I see the book as a boat now adrift, now at anchor, that skirts abysses; the holes and the chasms are also part of the whole. *Where am I?* is its name. It may make for land somewhere, each time it gets close, it veers off so quickly I'm afraid we're going to break, I never flee it, it often seems to me that it is under the influence of my mother's travelling soul, city-hopping as the winds of curiosity dictate, Isaac too moves between Berlin Cairo and Calcutta to Chicago.

At any moment, I can find my mother between Paris and Osnabrück.

I understand that the book like any true voyage governed by nostalgia is perpetually intensely anachronic.

Such is the destiny of characters expelled from their native place by violence and wars.

The minute Ulysses arrives in a port, hardly has he had time to refresh himself than he is off again: he recounts his stay in another port.

If he is in Algiers, he is at that very moment in Athens. No borders separate the two theaters.

Only Marcel has never left his dog. He was born with the animals. In my coffin, I want there to be photos of all the dogs I have loved.

Marcel has a dog which is itself a Marcel. I'm coming, he says. And here he is.

July 18, 2017: short conversation with Marcel

—Today I put you in my book.

—What book?

—The book I am writing. With my dead. With those I have loved and those I love.

—With my name?

—With your first name, the real one.

A smile flits across his lips, surprises Marcel, fades quickly, anxious to protect the dignity of the chief. Marcel is happy to be in a book. According to the knightly code of honor, one doesn't show one's emotions. This is courtesy. The more violent the emotions the more discreet they remain.

—And my dog?

—And your dog.

With your name and your dog. I wouldn't like to risk giving the impression that you are a fiction.

Your date of birth?

—March 10, 1935. I was born in the middle of the Forest of Eden, all eleven children were. With the eleventh, we won the 1936 Cognacq-Jay Prize for the biggest family in all of France and that was me. Thirty-five thousands francs in those days. We bought two cows. Later we had up to thirteen.

Me too, I'm happy. At last! At last Marcel has arrived. I announce the news to my daughter: this morning Marcel entered the book. —Oh! That's good.

My daughter is the witness, she can tell me all she likes that Jacques (the fatalist) was surrounded by Marcels and Marcelles, nonetheless for a long time, I've feared displeasing him.

My life with him takes place only in the Forest. We never speak of the City or any city. I am his guest in his domain. With the beasts. He loves my mother. With my mother, one is in the company of beasts and babies. My mother too is a being with large practical hands. The large hands recognize one another.

The beauty of this man, who gives the name of Marcel a nobility I shouldn't like to deprive it of, is that of a weathered Greek statue with damaged joints. He has the lineaments of an emperor still. His empire is Nature, the nature that saved Rousseau and will outlive us.

Someone

who has never read a book-of-paper, who half-reads half-doesn't-read, each of them taking turns one week the cows one week school,

the whole of the Forest of Eden, poor-man's-ferns, they loved it the cows they knew where to go who knows where to go, who understands everything, knows everything, when he sits down to ruminate I put my arm around his thick neck I kiss his head, his cheeks, he laughs, I hug Marcel the dog, he has large eyes brimming with kindness, this is a fact, thoughts, according to whether they are somber or transparent, are what light up a gaze

and without which my books would not exist.

Before he attacks he studies the gate. The gate is Marcel's adversary. A robot in aluminum, its face is stubborn as a Teutonic chevalier its rust-proof lock thermoplastic lock stop and steel strike plate have rusted, it could care less about us, it is a perverse gladiator of a gate, Passion is the brand name—illegible, so we feel its ill-will. Who knows why. Except for some obscure technological spite, the inhuman soul of an age stripped of memory. How far we are from the Forest of Eden!

—It's not a piece of poop.

This is the first time I have heard Marcel express himself using antiphrasis. Therefore the situation is serious. I would be suffering torments had I not faith. In him alone.

Just as I see Philia the geometer plot her leap to my desk make her secret calculations measure height and distance, transmit the results to her spine, hind legs, and tail, launch the operation and bring it to completion with mathematical elegance

So I see Marcel calculate his assault. He will be victorious, it is written.

—What would Isaac say? He'd say, is he good-looking, your Marcel? I'd say, Yes. In my opinion, Marcel is good-looking. A little worn down. Work has broken him. He walks a little crookedly. His hips are rusted. His knees block, like the lock. Tinnitus cicada-buzzes his ears. He lifts hedges. He up-ends gates. He accompanies me to the industrial zone to buy a vacuum cleaner. He wears a clean, pressed, sometimes pink shirt when he leaps to my aid with his blue trailer. I am not his sister.

He is handsome as a man who has never lost the Forest of Eden.

—I'm reassured you say he's good-looking, Isaac says.

You can tell Isaac is jealous.

I have never mentioned Isaac to Marcel. What would be the point? Isaac is a genius of Cities. The forest is not interested in the City. The forest writes its history differently. I'll give you an example: Marcel's father harvested resin from pines. There is no such thing any more. The resin secrets have all gone to Portugal. The species is extinct. Marcel's species is endangered. Isaac's species too, but differently.

For fifty years, my house has been my writing refuge and hence on many occasions an anti-Isaac shelter, for the writing is more jealous even than Isaac; in order to follow it, it demands that one forget, unconditionally, father mother beloved child, at least for a time, and it is now one of the mystical places where I work at maintaining Isaac's Perpetual Presence, as in our other sacred places: Montaigne's Tower or the Twin Towers and after the Towers' death, Saint Paul's Chapel, which he didn't want to enter, Strasbourg Cathedral where we prayed each time and where my mother, having entered against her will, promptly exited through a side door.

—Fortunately I am not jealous, Isaac used to boast, I say to my son. And I believed him. All the same our life was buffeted by storms of jealousy. True jealousy, the kind that does not exonerate the jealous, that gnaws at hearts and transmits rage. Isaac's jealousy can be summed up, more or less, by the following list, which I don't want to present in chronological order as my master Henri Brulard would no doubt have done because in no case can I fix a date, the storms were always unpredictable. Nothing let me foresee his outbursts.

In alphabetical order: A (the only person I thought I could love in the place of Isaac)

my friends

Frédéric

Helmut

Jacques

Jean

The President of the Republic

Rajeev

Here I add "Beethoven," the hero of one of my books under whose name Isaac sees a succession of floppy-haired candidates. Really I was intimate with none (masculine) of these suspects I say; none (feminine) of these suspects, I add. I love Isaac and Isaac alone, this one could be my son, that one is gay, Isaac is my sole desire. —As if that precluded a fling, does love heed propriety? Isaac growls, and I look at him apprehensively, —It's good Montaigne is dead, I say. —No jealousy is more cruel than jealousy of the dead. Do I know where you are when you sleep?

And when, worn out by trips and meetings, by the suffering one speaks of and the suffering one doesn't; when, fearful of the silences, passive, a victim, anguished, I seduce sleep with Lexomil, while you think I sleep and I do too, I meet you all in white like a department-store bride, and do you know who you are marrying, or pretending to marry!? That slut! I was utterly floored, a bride, all in white, in the most conventional manner, smelling of church, with that slut, and Saint Paul's into the bargain, how can you do this to me, leave me felled by the dragon and not wake me up. What have you done to me? I await an explanation.

But the worst, I say to my son, is the anti-jealousy. A sort of mute, cold, invisible jealousy, a specter, that can go to ground for decades, a slow virus no more detectable than herpes, then one midday, in January 2000, when we are sitting down to lunch in a charming guinguette on the edge of the Garonne, this is the bridge Montaigne took when he went to Bordeaux, where he should never have agreed to be elected mayor in 1581, do you recall our 1981, we had just resuscitated, you were coming from Rome where you couldn't not agree to be elected Prince of Poets, a burden all the more pleasant in that there is neither rent to pay nor wages other than the honor and sensation of being buried alive by so much praise—"*élu mais pas lu*," "elected but unread"—you tell me, and by the fleeting smile on your lovely pinched lips I read that in spite of yourself you were glad and secretly proud of being so honored, the sky before us was a fine dust of gold and I liked to picture the little man over there on his little horse trotting off to Parliament, and that's when

I don't know whether I was the one who knocked the glass of red wine over onto the tablecloth and thence to the trousers or whether it was him; or whether the glass fell over because of the violence of the attack or whether the spark that caused the powder keg of the unconscious to explode was the knocked-over glass and the red splash on the cloth and white trousers, is it the horror of blood on white, is it—I have no idea what is cause, what is occasion, what is metaphor, or perhaps it's

do you know what an eruption of burning lava is like when you don't see the volcano? I ask my son. And he says: —What happened with L. in 1981? And in 1968?

Stupefaction and panic, I tell my son, do you see what that means? I answer: 'Nothing' and this is the truth. Not much, nothing, and this is the truth. You don't halt an earthquake with Nothing. For thirty years, a fire smolders. For thirty years, a worm gnaws at the beams of the brain. And suddenly the roof bursts into flame and comes crashing down on us

or does the anguish engender an excess of happiness, that paroxysmal form of too-good-to-be-true of which Freud speaks, and following him L. or Othello's hysteria, or that pyre to which Dostoyevsky consigns his demon-love-possessed characters?

—How to explain this structure with two souls, this body with two hearts, the one confiding the other mistrustful? I asked my son the scientist. For in truth Isaac was not jealous fortunately.

—It's not a structure, my son says. It's different levels of the mind. At different depths, and therefore at the same time as at different times therefore not at the same time we are jealous on the ground floor, whereas up on the fifth we have never been jealous. Or vice versa. On the fourth floor you are affected. Down below, nothing. At the bottom, Isaac is not jealous. Up above, it's regarding the fourth floor, I say, at 54 rue Philippe in Oran, that was where Monsieur Émile the magician lived to whom I was apprenticed in 1940 and without whom it would never have crossed my mind that one can invent truths. I had just lost my first paradise and come into my first exile, overnight in a doomed military garden I had become a detritus, a spider, a roach, a piece of dirt, always about to be crushed by the powerful black machine of religions, I wasn't Catholic and I found myself ringed by streets off-limits to miscreants, at the corner of the Street of Jews and the Street of Rats, in my head windowless as a prison.

But on the 4th floor of the house besieged by an awfully bleak neighborhood lives Monsieur Émile who, like Helvetius for Stendhal, is to be my *predictor of things to come,* my master magician, first among the angels and doctors, with his

A Letter

"Halt!" says the book, "I have an urgent letter for you. *Excuse I interrupt you* but it's from Osnabrück." From the small peculiarities of its language I realize that the book has just landed in Germany. I'd planned to spend some time in Oran before coming back to New York. And now Osnabrück barges in. They're fighting over me. It occurs to me, I say to my daughter, that the book is jealous of itself. Just when I was getting settled in Algeria, I am cut off; you'd think that whatever happens to us down here "was written up there" that I am always going to be interrupted, after the model of the book of interruptions, the one that keeps wresting the right to speak now from Jacques now from his master, 340 times at least, so in the end there is no more master to speak of, except for the book.

And all because while I was being born in Oran, my mother was giving birth to me in Osnabrück. This originality explains why my book and I move in zigzags. Scene after scene. Occasionally one of the books' books makes a scene.

—As if I could have forgotten you, Osnabrück!

—I'm writing you from Osnabrück in Johannesburg, says the book. In English therefore. "What happened to Jacques's loves?" the fatalist asks on page 235.

"I am writing a book about the modernist South African architect Kurt Jonas (1914–1941). In one of your books I am excited to discover that my protagonist is a relative of yours. But I see that the Jonas family came from Osnabrück originally. I had always thought Kurt's father Moritz Jonas was from Osnabrück until another architect and genealogist informed me that the Jonases are from Borken and therefore related to Hans Jonas the philosopher. It all goes back to the eighteenth century when Meyer Jonas, born in 1790, the son of Benjamin Jonas who had been *a textile trader* in Langenberg since 1750 settled in Borken in Westphalia where he became *a cattle dealer and butcher*. According to another of my colleagues, however, Dr. H. van Pels of Amsterdam, everything started in 1739 in Bacharach, which Abraham Jonas, born in 1700, is said to have fled with his wife Sarah Rosalie Jonas, also his cousin, in the nick of time to avoid being accused of ritual murder, in the middle of the night in a boat up the Rhine, to hide with a cousin or with a paternal or maternal uncle in Gemen according to one version, in Borken according to another, and from thence to Osnabrück, or perhaps Langenberg, but not to Frankfurt where a medical-doctor uncle may have given them money to seek refuge further away. This is the same Abraham Jonas who is said to have been the model for the character whose Jewish odyssey Heine traced in his tale *The Rabbi of Bacharach*, merely modifying the dates of events, setting them in the Middle Ages, although they were modern, no doubt to avoid censure. My colleague, a Heine specialist, was able to consult the Heine archives. As you know, the poet's tale is brutally cut off following the loss of some chapters, according to Heine's own testimony. In fact, the documents about this loss are conserved in the archives. The real Abraham was not a rabbi but *a textile trader*, weaver and dyer. Heine took another liberty: Sarah the beautiful cousin-spouse was not sterile. Quite the contrary. She brought three or four children into the world during their long exodus, of whom at least two were adopted by Jonas family relatives.

"In 1846, the family took the name of Jonas for once and for all. Until then they kept switching. Are the Jonases Jonases? Do you think that they thought they descended from Jonas—or Jonah—the First, who was born in a whale, or who was raised by a whale, as legends have it? Is there a relationship between the various Jonas nomadisms and architecture or philosophy? It was in Borken that the extended Jonas family established its numerous businesses, it's not-inconsiderable reputation, they became municipal officials and counsels to the community. But the best is that Kurt Jonas is the third cousin of Hans Jonas (1903–1993) whose family was among the great textile merchants that had prospered in Borken since 1815. Whereupon Moritz, the father of Kurt, the son of Abraham Jonas (1826–1915, Borken) the tanner and Helene Meyer (1841–1926, Osnabrück), left for Johannesburg, but not his brother Salo, he had a number of them, whose sons Horst, Werner, and Fred, politically very far to the left, for there was a sprinkling of communists in the family, including Hans Jonas, not the other Hans Jonas, the philosopher, Hans Jonas the communist, the other one, and two sisters, maybe more, who made it to South Africa, Jenny whose son Walter Seehof was the founder and owner of the Seehof Department Stores of Johannesburg, and Paula who married Herbert Loewenstein who was a Johannesburg wool merchant, and just imagine, dear Professor Cixous, that Borken could be located in Osnabrück if not in reality, then in imagination or in a phantasm, your maternal great grandfather being the grandfather of Kurt Jonas, the subject of my book, and therefore, via adjacency, the grandfather of my book"

By the end my head is spinning, I feel I've lived two hundred years in twenty minutes, I would happily faint dead away like the lovely Sarah who resorted to swooning in order to avoid the unlivable scenes, I feel I've lost my house along with my reason; a diabolical dance with hundreds of Jonases sarabands me right to the Rhine, ah! I am full of nostalgia for my little Hase and my solid Osnabrück City of Peace; besides, I tell my daughter, all these Jonases are Jonases from Rhineland from North Westphalia, only our Jonases are Hanover Jonases, give or take a few kilometers

How simple and orderly everything is in the land of the dead when Ulysses descends to Hades, yes, of course they push and shove but this is nothing, each of them is in control of his story and his feelings while for us all is chaos and confusion, I tell my daughter. Who keeps a prudent distance from the bubbling Rhine and its banks.

A violent wish to escape seeps like terror through my body; for someone who must and has to write, all these family Jonas stories that melt one into the other, all these amputated, buried, kidnapped, substituted tales—it is the Flood. Heine too took to his heels.

Was Moritz Jonas Onkel Moritz Jonas or another? And Aunt Paula born in 1878 or in 1880 who couldn't be Aunt Paula born in 1883 since my grandmother Omi her little sister was born in 1882, Paula who died in 1942 although surviving, was she in London, and then who, who was in South Africa, was it Paula or not?

Who am I to say that so-and-so is a relative, this Jonas is a Jonas, that Jonas is he a Jonas? I understand why Jonas threw himself into the whale. Still, one cannot swallow such a crew

What I can tell you about South Africa in March 2008, my mother says, is owing to these 1998 letters I'm about to answer, letters from South American cousins to whom I am going to write that I am still here in March 2008, time flies, that is the twins Hans und Peter. My cousin Ellen Jordan told them, I beg you one stays with me the other left for South Africa, she was my mother and Onkel Moritz's niece. Her husband had a store that sold neck ties, in 1935 they left for South America with the four children the next day her husband died. She telegraphed Onkel Moritz of South Africa, can you lend me a little money, with that and his benediction she raised the four children. The one I saw, I saw him in Asuncion, he was very nice, it was raining cats and dogs. I put my plastic-airplane-vomit-bags on my head. I took them from the plane. Time flies. I did receive a letter from South Africa, but I don't know where it's gone.

And all these abandoned, unfinished tales, these cast-up chronicles buried under salt or sand, all these dead people whose ends are lost, how to think about them? Is there a kind of thought with the force to think about such scatterings?

Interruption is the specificity of Jewish genealogies, says my daughter, the hallucinatory effects of the homonymy.

But not all the Moritz Jonases go to Johannesburg, I say. I cling to the existence of Uncle Moritz as to a piton. Besides, Omi, her sister Rosi, took the plane in 1962 to go and visit Moritz in Johannesburg, he was there, I cling to this flight, I cling to the end of the Algerian war, and already Kurt Jonas, the well-known architect the Osnabrück South African had been dead for twenty years during the previous war, but my mother never mentioned that, she spoke to me about the Kurt Jonas who died in a concentration camp, whereas Kurt Jonas is dead of death, and it was of the other death, the death of the world, to which my mother bore witness. But Kurt Jonas of Johannesburg returns to Osnabrück in 1918, with Moritz, at the end of another war, to reunite with his old mother (Helene Meyer), my great grandmother, that is, and if my mother doesn't mention something, it's because it doesn't make any impression on her or that there is only one Kurt, or that she mistakes one for the other. In the end, my mother herself, my sole witness, had a role in the confusion, she confused Selma with Paula or Jenny.

Here I see proof that often it is not the human agent that matters in our tales, the principal protagonist is destiny, or events. After all it is not Ulysses, the person, who ties us to *The Odyssey*, but the sum of his adventures, and that they be really and truly finished, and that the end be domiciled.

"Do we lead destiny or does destiny lead us?" my captain was saying, said Jacques. The Fatalist.

Him, Jacques, the book, was cut off 108 times in a tale composed of 21 stories. Hard to say whether this is a lot, or a little. The breaks don't stop the book from trotting along. He tumbles, breaks a knee. He gets fixed. And off he goes again.

—Aunt Paula? my mother says. What a funny apartment in Osnabrück, you'd think it had been built by a dealer in bric-a-brac, the sitting room gave on the street, lord knows whose idea it was to put three stairs up to the kitchen and three more to the WC. You've got two windows on the street. In front there's a rostrum. In front of which is an *Erker*. On this corbel is a chair-to-look-into-the-street. My grandmother would spend the day there. One day she sees my friend Tony Kantor with my bicycle crash down in front of the big military horses. So much for the bike. Later there was the tram. The cousins from Gemen would spend the day on the tram. I'm going to see the seamstress, the neighbor says: What?! You're going to see that Catholic! Catholics lie, then they go to confession. They'd put two plaster angels in the sitting room between which you had to walk, whose idea was that? My grandmother claims they come from the Bacharach cousin. There's a *Kachelofen* you heat with briquettes. Behind the dining room is a windowless room where I sleep. I lay an ear to the wall. On the other side's a cafe, at night I hear music. Back then everyone rouged their cheeks. I had an aunt who did that in secret, she got it all over the place, she would hide if she saw herself. Aunt Paula. Aunt Paula—always looking for her keys. One day she'd left them in the chicken coop. Aunt Paula was a touch naive. She didn't dare spend the day on the tram but you could see she thought about it. —I wanted to paint you a portrait of Paula, it's all mixed up, no head no tail, in the end that's just like her.

Whereupon it occurs to me that my book is the result of this Jonas turmoil, haunted as it is by so many passengers and populations so foreign to one another, nowhere affiliated, forever moving on, fast-talking like Jacques and my mother and her sister, all astonished by its harlequin colors and everywhere torn, which pleads for a very distant and indeterminate kinship with the city of Bacharach whose constitution is so extravagant, disheveled, wild, unlikely, it defies all claims to reality and yet it exists, and yet its historical and physical frenzy, its daily delirium really did rout a poet as agile, courageous, and well armed as Heine, and it took a Victor Hugo to lead Bacharach instead of Bacharach leading him.

—Bacharach? Victor Hugo says. You'd think a giant, a dealer in bric-a-brac wanting to open a shop on the Rhine, took a mountain for his shelves, and arrayed there from top to bottom, with his giant's taste, his collection of outsized curios, it starts under the surface of the Rhine, even. There, tip emerging, is a volcanic rock, according to some, a Celtic peulven, a Breton menhir, according to others, a Roman altar. . . . Then, on the edge of the river, two or three old ship hulls that fishermen use as shacks.

—*Bacharach,* my mother says, you've read it?

The whole time my mother was living and reading I didn't read *Bacharach,* it was written that I would not read *Bacharach,* thou shalt not read, she who could read such a book would discover the power and courage it required for someone to write such a book, I am not that person, I am not a giant

the volumes of *Heinrich Heines Sämtlicher Werke in Zwölf Bänden* parade in black battledress across Eve's bookshelf as if on a mountain since the Middle Ages in order to keep me from staring at Bacharach, daubed with a war paint of gothic letters that render indecipherable a pell-mell of droll sentences, bijou sentences turreted sentences with embossed facades, impossible gables from whose interlinear double staircases bell towers shoot up like the asparagus in each of the paragraphs of a text by Proust, weighty beams that speak Montaigne's Latin, inscribing delicate arabesques on cabins, spiral granaries, lit corbels, faience stoves in the form of crowns, puffing philosophical smoke, and extravagant weather vanes more like capital letters cut out of sheets of tin, cookie-cutter cut-outs that wince in the wind of a quill pen.

But when my mother asks, Bacharach, you know it?

I say, yes, no, of course not, overhead I hear a *B* an *a* a *ch* taking their time speaking up, for all literature crowds into this name, halls of mirrors out of some fairytale, encrusted with tiny archivolts and picturesque, gemstone syllables.

To live in Bacharach is to live in a magic formula. A giant swarming with dwarfs. No one can read Bacharach, I tell my daughter, except Victor Hugo and my mother, and except

Bacharach is the story the Jonases inhabited before the bloodshed. In Osnabrück too, there are no more Jews. The Jonases have gone up in philosophical smoke. Of the old days what remains in these towns is something fairytalish, an ambient chemistry that awakes an irresistible urge to recount. Is it the churches' rivalry, the towers, the ruined synagogues, that are, after all, the monumental crystallization of human dreams, the turning into stone of vain hopes and ambitions?

And sometimes all the volumes of an all-but-finished work like Proust's lead to a poignant desire for a cathedral-book

for a cathedral remains unfinished only in order to open its arms to the next poet.

Bacharach is the most beautiful true hallucination that Victor Hugo ever transcribed under the dictation of the spirits. It's his Rhineland Divine Comedy. Given that the visit happened in a dream, it is both gigantic and brief like a stroke of genius. In the end there is no end. The poet sets one foot in the tomb, and he is wafted off to heaven like Isaac on the elevator that carries us at the speed of light to the edge of the clouds.

Finally I call my son on the telephone, the son in his other world where all is order and beauty. —Do you know about Bacharach?

A tohu-bohu of sounds, I was shouting: Bacharach! Ra cha ra— Ah brouhaha! I know about Brouhaha! hollers my son. Baruch Habba! Blessed is He who comes, it is the racket of benediction of He who comes beshem Adonaï who comes from the Lord. Brou! Blessed be the racket of He who comes. No event without Barouhaha —Bacharach! I shouted. Oh, Bach?! whoops my son, Bach the musician? —So I shout: no, the rabbi, but maybe he is a musician. It is a novel. It traces a rabbi's path from brouhaha to brouhaha, —You are telling the tragedy of Baruch the rabbi without God whose love life was a comedy? —I hadn't thought of it, but the Book remembers. It commences with a flight. The legend of the rabbi-who-flees. And do you know how it ends? I've forgotten, but even Proust remembers. Nerval too. It doesn't end. Baruch, blessed be the one who flees. You just have to be ready. To flee. Which happens.

There is a city whose name flees. Despite its name the city exists. In the Rhineland. It was invented in the nineteenth century, contemporaneously with Osnabrück. There, there was an Abraham Jonas, the first Jonas fugitive in the vast Rhine region, who fled when he found that he was about to be accused of ritual murder. Flight has been in the family ever since. The archives show that each time the Jonases settled down forever in this or that city or in a village, the time between settling and flight was on the average two generations. The Bacharach Jonases were tolerated, that is not tolerated, until the end of the Great Plague, the sixteenth-century one that was imputed to the Jews, hence some forty years.

The Osnabrück Jonases put down roots in 1881; by 1901, it is generally accepted that they were already among the town notables, says my mother, they had nine children and a flair for business. They built homes for the future, which ended with Hitler, by 1935 it was already over, by 1942 all those who had believed were dead, as for me by 1930 I was in another story, by 1935 in Algeria, I liked my little bric-a-brac apartment Oran-Osnabrück very well—until 1972 when I took one suitcase and the next plane out of Algiers for anywhere. I call this not missing an opportunity to flee.

When I consider the exceptional longevity of my existence in the country from which I write, I am forced to recognize that I am not a typical Jonas. Why am I so sad? *Ein Märchen aus alten Zeiten das Kommt mir nicht aus dem Sinn*

—Do you know *Bacharach*? I put the question to Isaac, it crosses my mind that he could pursue the construction that Victor Hugo following Heine carefully left unfinished. Bacharach? —Bacharach? It's the metro station whose tortuous name we couldn't get when we got lost in Brooklyn as in a fairytale? I remember, a neighborhood in Jerusalem, where I got lost and which was as empty as a dream. I was hunting for the name of a spell. Susimin! Sumsum! Arbadak arba. Abraca dabra. Bacharach in Hebrew means 'I am lost four times over.' In the Hebrew of my dreams.

Bacharach, I say, you say the name and already you have an entire book, a book like a city that calls and wants to enchant you like a Lorelei.

—It's Manhattan's secret name in our personal history.

If there are books that are like cities created at the call of a beautiful rose cathedral, there are cities that are like books, that expand, that grow in height and depth, that become storehouses of Time, that open lovely, troubling cemeteries and guide us to our tomb in order to help us tame it, right up until it becomes our secret hotel room, our solitary confinement

No one knows Bacharach and yet Bacharach exists

When I wanted to call the Book *Bacharach*, Isaac was firmly opposed; as it is, you are pretty illegible, think of your reader. *Osnabrück* was already a lot, it's like Cixous, all of that is steep, abrupt, strange not to say foreign, I worry about you, take my advice; and in this he agrees with my mother. —Who'll want to read about a bizarre little city stuck between the cliffs of the Rhine and totally inaccessible except by boat, they're going to think you've made it up again, whereas you could be writing best-sellers, a name like that, a dead end, do you know the expression?

Remarque didn't exhibit the name of Osnabrück either, had he called *All Quiet on the Western Front Osnabrück*, the book wouldn't have sold like hotcakes, says my mother, he speaks of Osnabrück to the entire world without ever speaking that impossible name, nobody's making you who's going to notice if you change a name.

Doomed Staircases

—My books are cities in which Morpheus dwells. My poets are all dead. The dead still live in the cities that yesterday they cast their spell over. Ghosts? my daughter asks. Time's guardians, I say. —Guardians of the Temple. Whatever the day, Monsieur Émile still waits for me on the fourth floor of the rue Philippe, we are on the second floor, the German-Jewish floor with my father tall and long as an African stork turned into a young doctor, on the third floor my slow, immemorial Spanish grandmother, motionless, waiting for grief's colic, shifting from her stomach to her lower back, to rise at last with a sour violence to her throat, suddenly her black marble statue cracks, then the relief of bellowing, retching, ululating—my son what have you done to me! So do you like your new apartment? You are happy there on the ground floor? You are at peace, right? And no sheet. No telephone. While my father is being reduced to compost and from his substance the grass grows tall, no one is allowed to approach, this is her grazing ground, he's her calf, she bends over my father who is no longer my father but her son her flesh her meat her anger, and woe betide anyone she catches spying.

—Hands off these bones, you bad girl!

You can't fight her hunger, my grandmother's appetite is sacred

—Watch out! I'll give you what for, headache!

As soon as she sees what's in my mind, behind her dentures the threats begin to rumble she's got her eye on me

eventually I will realize that it is Georges and only Georges she adores, a monotheistic furor

—And your husband, Mémé? I should ask in Spanish, but it's foreign to me; her mouth full of earth, she doesn't answer.

To her son she expresses her hunger, he's the adored the hated the abandoner. For the husband no cemetery, my grandmother climbs to the fourth floor.

Come in. The apartment itself has not changed. This is where Monsieur Émile turns little by little, with Alice, into eternity and Alice with Monsieur Émile her meager other half also her brother turns into eternity, although more silently more in the alchemical depths, unfathomable too but bubbling away in her enormous retort, under the for-me-unimaginable coils of her flesh whose quantity and volume would suffice for the three people, in all Oran nobody is as vast and consequential in form and weighty mystery as Alice, appended to Monsieur Émile

the two of them form one androgynous being, to all appearances what the one lacks is the lure of the other, in the beginning there was the last wish of Madame Carisio their mother: you shall not imprison yourselves in marriage and when I'm dead don't think I won't have an eye on you, and ever since; that is, for fifty years, ever since 1940 when I discovered the fourth floor, her Last Wish has reigned over the apartment, to each his share of fidelity, Monsieur Émile remains sterile and hence as paper-thin as Don Quichotte, Alice conserving in her fleshy envelope all the children she hasn't had, right to the last dilation determined by the size of the dining room. Thus far and no further. Once Alice the humungous is seated for six in the corner of the dining room, the visitors and Monsieur Émile share the rest of the room.

—Microbe! my father calls her, and everyone thinks this is the right way to address Alice, the is the way to name someone whom a spell has turned into maxi-fairy.

Madame Carisio's spirit is content. You can feel it breathing throughout the apartment, in the twin faience dogs fiancéed to the faience cats on the faience mantel in a harmony of mandarin and blue.

For lack of space, Monsieur Émile and Alice sleep in the same bed. There is also the mandarin cat. And the rat. The rat that bit Monsieur Émile in his sleep. The proof? His right earlobe is missing. As a result, he always seems to see the rat nibbling at its morsel. And the cat? Didn't bite the rat. A good-for-nothing cat, my mother says. Monsieur Émile is the one who chased the rat.

Saturdays they descend to the third floor to lunch chez les Cixous. The remarkable thing is that the Carisios are Catholic and the Cixous are Jewish but their attachmentfusion is so anciently and philosophically astonishing that no one notices this. During the meal, the Catholics and the Jews are converted into one another. Everyone eats garlic ratatouille. Except Omi my German grandmother.

At 54 rue Philippe everything is double just as in *A Midsummer Night's Dream* in reality as in a dream as in reality, going up and down between the floors in the reality of the dreams and the dreams of reality. Here one receives the dead and here one receives the animals. A place is set for theosophy and spiritualism on the third and fourth floors, this makes Omi laugh, on the second floor superstition is scorned.

Alice and Monsieur Émile are brother-and-sister Pharmacists in the Urgent Pharmacy, Monsieur Émile invented *Pharmakon* a mandarin-flavoured liqueur with which he could have made a fortune, my mother says, it's damnably intoxicating, but why doesn't he advertise it? This too Madame Carisio senior has forbidden, they are content to be celibate magicians.

I am six, outside the war is on, I was sitting on Monsieur Émile's lap, he gives me a sip of *Pharmakon*, I understand those who can't stop drinking, it is divine. Monsieur Émile tells me his extraordinary tales, I am drunk on his fantastic liqueurs, I swallow everything for real.

And in the armchair in the mirror I see my very beautiful and very noble German grandmother watching us, *bei uns* in Osnabrück chez nous *one doesn't believe* in fairy tales, says Omi, in Osnabrück my grandmother forbade us to read fairy tales, my mother says. The fairies fled to the stairwells and attic.

I belong to Monsieur Émile pharmacist magician I want his made-up stories and I want to believe them

It is here on the fourth floor, despite the reserves expressed on the second, that I acquired a taste for the liqueur of writing, I say to Isaac. On the fourth floor it is possible to believe what one doesn't believe for a few hours, even a whole day, not-believing doesn't keep one from believing, it is an enchantment of the senses, underneath the speech of the magician I sit and there are two of us on his lap, she who believes and she who secretly doesn't, this is not a problem, we get along fine, today the bells ring, the sirens howl, the alert Monsieur Émile has donkey ears, forgive me my little rat I didn't have time to change my ears this morning, I went fishing with Oberon, the cafe owner, on his boat I am a donkey but I brought back a bucket of sardines for all my Oran cats. Monsieur Oberon cafe boss fisherman is Spanish too. He is a catholic Catholic. Monsieur Émile, the Spanish magician is a Jewish

Catholic. He believes in the resurrection of cats. *Quatsch*! my German grandmother exclaims.

Yet in Bacharach they believed in spells. But from Bacharach to Osnabrück the road runs through the Enlightenment.

We are spirits of another sort. *But we are spirits of another sort*, Isaac says.

On this page we may ascend to the stars on the 107th floor to clink glasses with the dead while sipping some Love Juice concocted in the Oran Pharmacy, and from the terrace see what will happen in a hundred years when Isaac's hair will have grown into dozens of tight silvery ringlets. This is what happens when I listen to Monsieur Émile's tales, no longer is there a single present that twines the past with the future. From the terrace sometimes you can glimpse Manhattan's towers.

In Oran the stars hang over the fourth floor. From the terrace sometimes you glimpse Jerusalem. We are on a plateau with no guardrail and a view over the green-gold circle of the seven mountains. My grandmother hangs out her washing on this plateau and from it I watch the future approach. A moment's inattention and Elpenor falls to his death. There is no chimney. I wonder how Father Christmas gets in, for he doesn't come from the street. He disembarks directly at Alice and Monsieur Émile's. All that cannot happen on the second floor happens on the fourth, at the magician pharmacists, Hotel des Revenants

On Sunday, my widowed Spanish grandmother goes upstairs for news of her husband. Since his death Alice has been the postmistress. He dictates letters to her, preferably on Saturday night. In his letters he says that all is fine and he quotes Victor Hugo. Now he has time to read all those giant volumes by the giant that in his lifetime he never opened what with the work in the shop and each tome's superhuman weight, he never even thought about it. P.S. I advise you to buy a lottery ticket with Alice. She knows the number. Still the same, my grandmother thinks. The lottery is not her thing. She doesn't buy a ticket. The letter suffices. She doesn't believe in Santa Claus

The letter has no spelling mistakes, she notices. Since it's Alice who takes it down. —Alice, could you leave my husband's spelling mistakes, pls?

It's as if Alice had washed her husband's feet. My grandmother thinks and doesn't say. The two women move slowly, heavily, around the table, like full-bellied whales who convert the green salt of truth into yellow gold.

It is Sunday, the floor-washing bucket is awash in sardine heads, Monsieur Èmile and I, heart beating as if I were off to a black mass or to the vicinity of Hades, go to Létemps Garden to feed the cats that come running to the plane trees, their drooping heads recovering a little strength at the sight of the fish heads, a first image sacrificed to the feeling of pity, I hate going to feed the cats, not all the sardines in the world will suffice to relieve the hunger that devours their stomachs and me too at the sight of them I utter horrible cries of abandoned cats, terror fills my eyes with tears we set the heads down on sheets of newsprint, the world is populated with on earth the disinherited and in the air, the dead, every Sunday the skeletal cats wait for the Messiah, Monsieur Émile has come down to earth to hear the woe of the cats and the dead

This book too has several floors. There are days the tale pauses at the Enlightenment, others when the Bureau of Dreams awaits us, yet others in the inferno of the camps

What draws us towards the Tower's peak is not the promise of the view for so high up we no longer see our everyday world but the promised-refused one that was granted Moses as his infernal damned grace. So what is it? my daughter asks.—I'm thinking, I say. It is an otherworldly strength. I find: *it's the presentiment.* There are presentiment places and days and hours too. You are in the staircase which is the Staircase, the medium, the familiar and the fateful, and all of a sudden inside you, you "see" the mystery that is a mixture of death and eternity. Or of eternity and death. And its heart is the diamond of life. For it is in the heart of this mixture, an atmospheric mixture of other worlds, that life sparkles and shines.

—Do you remember Hamlet's fateful Stairs? The Stairs in which he nearly falls three times, *as he descends,* and going back up, he feels he has no more memory, nor thought, nor strength, nor any existence, I couldn't care less if they come to name me king or Nobel Prize winner, Isaac says. I am ready. *The readiness is all.* I am ready, ready for anything. *I shall win at the odds.* Life—it's whatever happens in the Stairs.

Presentiment Is

Sometimes I'd hide us in the Gramercy Hotel, not because of the excellence of the hotel but because of its name, its name of promise and pardon, its fictional name, Isaac with me, my mother with her sister; I trusted providence to keep the universes separate. There were no collisions. It was as if we were running through different hourglasses

—The world in which you lived with him, is not yours, is not his, is not mine, my son says, it is yours, yours in the plural. In this world "between the two of you" there was no place for your worlds without him or his worlds without you.

The cab driver is a Sikh, en route for Brooklyn. —Where to? —Brooklyn. —Where in Brooklyn? —The Jewish neighborhood. We are going to get lost. Off we go, it's a long drive we come to an empty intersection, Williamsburg, here it is, complete and utter depopulation.

The main street is as deserted as if its residents had gone away or gone to ground, as if we'd come along belatedly, as a gleam of embarrassment flickers on, as if we were the two last rats on board after the shipwreck, then all of a sudden men and boys in talliths and large felt hats pour into the street, we get out, we go after them, now we are in the fifteenth century, we look around, five centuries from now we will be in the same street, it is that time of day, the time when they come out of the temple, who would have thought there were so many, the old man is stronger and more resistant than the youngsters, they are coming out, I ask a felt hat: —May we enter? —*No*. —This big *No* is well worth a letter from Victor Hugo but I don't have his pomp and splendor in me, this No requires the amplitude of his *Legend of the Ages*, it drops like a rock on the serpent's tongue. No one has ever received such a majestic No. Isaac says: women aren't allowed, remember? As if he himself were not, for the moment, a kind of woman. We walk for a long time, Lee Avenue is a street where I wouldn't be surprised to see a camel sway past, but an endless flow of Jews descendants of Jews into Jews since Galilee, boys with beards and shaved heads, black suits white shirts, Bacharach minus the festivity no cars, we could have been, we can't deny we have something in common, we cannot not deny, it is Saturday, we want to go back to Room 624, melt into each other, nourish the desire that cries like a newborn, we are stared at, undesirable, untranslatable

death began here, but we didn't know

—Presentiment, my mother says, is when you get a letter and think it is not for you

it's like for the Shavuot fire, my grandmother it was her birthday all eight grandchildren were coming to Osnabrück, all of a sudden there was a fire in the coal cellar no one wanted to tell her it was a minor holiday when one was not allowed to light a fire

so who started the fire, who wrote the letter?

Baruth the agnostic rabbi wanted to smoke. What happens? He goes down into the street and he waits

meanwhile, my mother compares religions, each sins and cheats differently, in any case the pope hasn't resolved the priests' problems with pedophilia, I think he was masturbating says my mother in any case there's no way to suppress that kind of urge, what hypocrisy perhaps someone will have the courage to marry the priests the Jews marry off their young very early, they know what they are doing, except Baruch who died in the end without ever having married, on holidays he had to go down to the street if he wanted to smoke a cigarette, maybe they take them to the bordello first, their fathers, perhaps this is not officially authorized

and in the end what happened? A gentleman with a lit cigarette comes along. —Sir, do you have a light? The Gentleman gives him a box of matches. So Baruth sees that the Gentleman is also a Jew who has faith problems. So do you know what happened? The matches end up setting fire to the coal cellar. We never knew how, everyone lied to my grandmother, that it was poor Maria, a nice housemaid who set the fire, they all had lovers who stole their pennies, that's what happened to the poor girls, they had children they had to abandon, they were impeccable spellers and geographers, in summer she worked in the fields, in another story I discover that Baruth could have married her, but having an idea like that is tantamount to setting fire to the coal cellar. And the second time do you know what happened? The Nazis set fire to the cellar. That was the last straw, I didn't wait. Right after that

All Quiet on the Western Front

But to return to our tower

Never have we been so close to heaven. From here I can imagine Siegfried and Kriemhild going to the most joyous, the biggest festival of any bible, Shavuot times two thousand, they ascend all the avenues festooned with our memories, on Central Park Avenue their enthusiasm knows no bounds, the inventory of their joys takes exactly two hundred stanzas you sense the poet is close to asphyxia like a cantor whose shofar won't stop, that day all mourning is forbidden, if you've lost a relative, no sorrow, keep your tears for next week, after the hoopla and the holy mass of childhood memories, we return to the hotel I turn on the television, thus far I am still in Paris the book, I think, is coming along with me but here it shoots ahead like a missile

I still don't believe what is already as clear as the nose on my face, the room is on fire, the bed glows red with the smoke, and in a moment I see what I see

Those are our Towers! Our Towers! They are killing our Towers! Our Towers are us! Wake up, Samson! Your Towers have been sheared! Imagine his horror! No, my imagination lacks the force to imagine. The little man lies under the ruins of Strasbourg Cathedral! They are killing our cathedral!

I call you or you call me. Where are you? In your hotel my day is your night.

you cannot imagine the malaise I feel in my chest here in the region of my heart, *but it is no matter*

our secret restaurant is closed, we should not have gone to just one restaurant, that's life, it is like our Towers, we only have one, we'll find another

the feeling that we'll never go there again, *it is but foolery,* but still in the airplane and at dinner in the evening his knee touching my knee. And on the blue shirt the branchy blue tie, although fatigue, insomnia, anxiety

and Sunday hearing of the death of Lokenath Bhattacharya, drown oneself in the Nile, so close to heaven, dizziness, vomiting. Or am I suffering from another world? Day imitates nightmare, but still, we are alive, the poets are dying this year but not all the stars all the same

a tooth, up top, near another one that is threatened too I don't know if this has to do with the tooth, one day or another—all that region there, unfortunately, one after the other, they fall, it's better to . . . , Isaac says

it's better . . . to be . . . deaf—tower?—deaf! you can always get another tooth . . . this is something I think about every day, how I accept, despite, because of, at the news of the death of Montaigne, I wept,

I accepted it, if the word philosophy means anything, philosophy in the sense of wisdom but I know poets who do not become philosophers, they have all their teeth and they tear the assassins of poets to pieces with their steel pliers,

interrupt everything, go away, stop America, love, write a terrible letter from Paul (Celan) to Ingeborg, too tired farewell! *Fooleries*, all this craziness, I'm counting on you to look after my teeth. Me I will look after your eyes and the cat, Isaac says

here I am looking after his teeth, never has the anguish so disheartened me, next she prays, she asks for the help of what serves her as God, and the following Tuesday he comes, he comes on time, he returns to the Hotel of love, well come, dark blue shirt, I clasped you in my arms my fiancé my fiancée, how I wanted you, hopelessly, how I hoped without hope, how I tried to incline my soul, I lave his soul with my tongue I lick his soul right to the belly, right to the neck,

Thea the cat queens it over our bed when he came on her, she was calm, firm, confident, I said go away Thea go away, I'm afraid I'll fall on you while he's pushing in me in all directions and without hesitation, *we defy augury* she says, she does not withdraw *not a whit*, to be, without hesitation, this is the way to go. To be. *There is a special providence*, a providence for each, all night I was not able to sleep, because of the anguish strapped around my heart, and now I sleep, I've slept nonetheless, the cat sleeps, he strokes her roughly rough gentleness, rough-gentleness, it is she in reality who is stroking him,

after that we always make love with the cat after that I fear for the cat too but this is foolishness

for an entire year *we defy the auguries*, the teeth seem to be OK, the cat is everywhere goddess on the desk her nose in the notebook in which I am writing stretched out on the telephone where your voice says me too me too, meowtoo Thea says, I defy the whole year fear, fearful, courage, the fearful feels, the teeth fall out anguish envelops the heart, never knowing if in fretfulness or reality

unending the auguries, the more one is afraid the more courage pushes back, Isaac, trembling, signs his letters "Thea," who cares about my fooleries, *we defy augury*!

—What time is it in Beijing? Is this you my China calling me? Are you calling me? —Don't go away! They're falling! We watch each other fall. In the dream they fall without cease, towers falling, falling can take a long time, scarcely turned to dust they pillar, around their stumps in a second forests veer to autumn, all crisp-around-the-edges autumn, the teeth of cats scatter like seed, the lovely swans that were a second ago are inchling runts the pillars are going to run away, towards the heavens, suddenly, there is no more fuel, no bird is able to fly, we watch all the world's tears fall, the Towers fall on Tuesday, all week, again forever

Stars that are the work of humans, you fall, Isaac says we are in the little wooden elevator in tears rocketing to the stars and there is no space, if that is all the good it does, Anafranil, then I can do without says Isaac, a terrible voice, happiness falls not feeling so great, good weather, bad weather the interpretation machine, a lot of dreams, I woke up Hitler was there among the others at breakfast he was still there I was in Beijing with Hitler, an extraordinary hotel, in fact, I need to be protected

—Don't go away! I'm watching on the television, it's beginning again, it will take a while for us to understand all the consequences, it feels personal to me, where is your mother? how is the cat?

Life is moving on commercial flights are taking off again, I saw Bush talking, under everything life goes on

my mother is in England, with her sister, she is being English, *nice weather nice travel lots of food* I never stop eating. *We are at the Docks,* extraordinary *we went to the British Museum,* in the evening we went to a good restaurant, the Empire State Building wasn't tall enough for them, *if you want to live happy live hidden, goodbye so long*

how many postcards! Towers the towers! Twenty-some!

The thought of a day when there are no more Postcards of the Towers, when? The end is nigh.

It occurs to me that somewhere far away that the machine of fearing and flying off again has already moved on, long before me. It makes my heart ache

I could care less about auguries. Fuck them. We are crazy, crazy. Henceforth I fear for us. But these are *fooleries*

You can replace teeth. Towers can be replaced. All but one. My soul is in Montaigne's Tower, sheltered

We pick ourselves up, we move on, within twenty-four hours planes take off again, bon appétit, my mother says, I'm off to eat my sauerkraut, in England? I say, tinned, says my mother. And you?

I leave my mother to her sauerkraut. I respect her sauerkraut. Her sauer-kraut amuses me, it is rich in signifiers, it even has room for a tower, and more than one, like my mother.

The Towers our deaths our dead how many deaths?

We need to add all the dead that the death of the Towers felled in the Stairwells of memory.

And you? my mother asks. What did you have for lunch?

What's new? Isaac asks. The deaths, I thought.

To the West, nothing new, Ecclesiastes says. Are the dead (not) news?

I'm rereading *All Quiet on the Western Front*, I say. It is the most beautiful book in the world. Listen once to this book and it will be with you forever, at six o'clock in the morning we take a break on page 108. Truce, grief's truce, the earth is crammed with half-living corpses the way the currents of the Scamander are so swollen with bodies it vomits them overboard, misery's brief truce, the dead fall silent like birds for the night, and the young soldier, his head bowed over the darkness, the young soldier to whom the war feeds daily massacres, here he is giving birth, like a young virgin mother, to Divine Poetry. Before him, no one, or only Homer. At six o'clock in the morning Homer wakes up in German for the first time in three thousand years. He is a little soldier a lyric poet from the city of Osnabrück recruited for Tragedy, like all nineteen-year-old prophets he doesn't know he has been chosen, which is why he has the grace of poets, he passes from childhood to eternity while taking life and death in a single bite, in the bloody breast of the great carnage the apocalypse is his schoolmaster, his Homeric name is Remarque, he was warned, according to my mother his family was so ill-housed that it was hardly housed at all, he wanted to leave for

America instead, war, without him no one would ever have brought back the dismembered speech of the dead, tender phrases with crushed knees, cut hands, and that one aposiopesis

finishes off

like the ghost of a howl,

"you . . ."

Between two attacks, the supernatural peace of writing, sitting beside the dead man who is for a moment still alive, has not yet digested the slice of sausage, has no intestines, is caught up in the infinite wisdom of the end: "report me" and the rest is silence for all these co-dying are Hamlet's successors, princes of mud and sorrow, "tell my story" and during the deep, fresh peace in between the rockets' thundering, now the ghosts of beloved landscapes appear, the gentle old poplars, along the gentle little river of the City, all those adorable fallen who will never again return in reality. And these two yellow butterflies that play for a whole afternoon in front of our trench,

who are they?

Their wings are dotted with red. They are so indifferent to the bombs, Tristan and Isolde, the space of a flight out of time in the forest that has replaced the world, no one could have invented these two spirits

And the beauty of the world recommences, and for the first time we discover Memory's America, and the world picks itself up weeping, and silent, for it comes back in images and in the thoughts that don't speak with words but with visions and lost landscapes.

No book can be more beautiful, more pure, more innocent, more washed in great blood, cherry red to begin, later charred. It responds as a desolate crowd to the slaughter of lambs. It is a human diamond. Blood is the secret. Each page is paid in cash with blood and all the different dying gurgles. Kropp and Westhus fall on page 108 and on the other side another soldier, headless, whose body survived an instant upright, like a madman.

There is only one poet, only one per inferno, to drag the remains of the astonished little men flung into the fire without explanation, without sense, without reason, like roses or tulips, into paper's cloister.

A little deeper into the forest, the soldier Klein, amazed, bends over his own body, which is slipping away from him, what terrifies him is his leg that is going, that has come undone, chopped off, his thigh stolen mute with horror while a dreadful pain chirps around his helmet then stops. From his feet to his knees, both of them, this one and that one, an icy solitude mounts to his belly, now it is in his chest so he lifts his coat over his face, shoves his helmet off that way he doesn't see that there is nobody near him to mourn and say farewell I'll look after you we'll see each other again, or my love, something that holds your hand

Remarque notes on page 114 that from afar in the voice that by the second day has lost its flesh and is now only a moan one hears the name of Rosi or perhaps Elise, a bit of a name, ise, osi

and as always the sky is blue without a cloud,

and the sadness grows, melancholy is blue, and when the soldier weeps, I feel that my own tears respond this is not a book, this tale, not a death not disposable not frozen it is not a thing, not even a tender and desperate song far off in memory, it is here here within me in my inner meadows in my wounded forests that it runs like a magnificent animal full of life and terror, a deer maybe, or a species of angel, wild and refined, it is more than a friend, a lover, the sort that is proud and poignant like a quadruped angel, to whom I am indissolubly tied as my heart is joined to the heart of my cat

The leg the cannonball blew off, was it the left or the right? I should have liked to know, so as to invoke Michael Klein, I miss that detail, I ought to have asked my grandmother, now I am short one leg for eternity, for that reason I can't hold a proper funeral for him, it's as if I didn't know which tower had been blown away first

I know that I can do nothing for Michael Klein my grandfather, I can do nothing for the fireman Eddie Starck FDNY Engine 7 whose smiling photo hangs on the side of Saint Paul's out of the dust with the wreathes surrounded by rotting wreathes, already rotting, the body fallen to ashes, and the rest is silence, I can do nothing for the photo, nothing against the photo which smiles at anyone going by, despite its condemnation to death, like a large friendly dog

And that's why Remarque's visit, so late, forever and never too late, I don't run into him in the street I meet him in this book, too late, or maybe not, perhaps it's the will of this book, maybe the last one

having skirted the walls of so many cities, towers, windmills on the river, prisons, for many years, here is Remarque at the door, I was expecting him already on page 37 then it was page 41, during the quasi-celestial Lunch with Isaac I ceased thinking about him, up there neither time nor war, so when? the Book asked, page 96 I say, at that moment he isn't far from us, a few streets, a few years away, nearby, ready, he takes Fifth Avenue towards Central Park it is very hot now, the sky is blue as an augury, on 70th Street all of a sudden it smells of Germany, he quotes Heine, Shakespeare, the Bible, in English with his Hanover accent, familiar, there is even the Bacharach Café, and the Hindenburg Café, and now the exile no longer knows where he is,

but that is good, *the readiness is all*

this Book already dreamed of receiving Remarque as principal ghost, before knowing its real title I sense the tie of the *sans* between us, the *sans* ground the *sans* passport the *sans* address the *sans* fear but not *sans* terror, and when there was the autodafé in 1933 in Osnabrück, even if I wasn't born, still I lived through it in my hallucination and horror the flames seemed to come from the Jonas house cellar and I trembled as if it were Remarque's work, Isaac's work flung onto the brazier as they tossed Bacharach's children onto the fire

—The ablation makes you write, says Isaac. A very light kiss in the elevator. The elevator, another of our Stairways, a sort of dream Stairway, condensed, too short, like life, a synecdoche of infinite love on our lips, our forehead, the str

the strange power of the miniature, the Twin Towers in a stamped envelope, a portrait of Isaac and me in Tours in the Towers

—The ablation makes you write, I tell Isaac. I look at him. And then I see him as this mixture of Isaac and the Towers that hurts here all around my heart

The jealousy was back on October 1, desire is this boy who plays in the ruins New York is still smoking it is six o'clock in the morning

—I tried everything, three cards, I buy cards, I call with my MCI card, busy, with my ATT card, still busy, no luck with SPRINT either. — I dreamed I was talking to you on the phone I say, it was my dream on the line. —Are you sure the line wasn't busy? There wasn't somebody with you? None of your reproaches or recommendations please, all by myself I am afraid enough

welcome, Jealousy, furious nymph of October 1, 2001, I won't complain today about your savage love letter, I don't hate you, refractory mirror of Isaac's soul, I won't ask Isaac if there was someone with him charming indifferent bacchante amid the din of ferocious and bellicose global Jealousy, love means embracing one another while laughing at the howling of the Tempest, a blind giant seeks in vain to squash two ants who are faster than death,

I welcomed with joyful tenderness the young the fresh the naive she-devil, so it all goes on, the cruel comedy has escaped the bombardment unharmed, bliss of the terrified who creep from the underground shelter, thoughts shake themselves off like children, so the fall of the Towers hasn't yet managed to damage us, yet in other tales of catastrophes, cataclysms, earthquakes, floods, novels, and bibles, things come to a sad end

upon which your revealing phone call,

(I hold onto these precious moments where Isaac, despite himself, offered up his secret, inner room where despite himself everything was avowed, where suddenly the flaw of his greatness was revealed)

I received the Towers. You have to imagine the apparition. This portrait of what had vanished at the height of their immortality, these photographs of Innocence. The Towers rising above time, continuing. I gave a cry of joy. It's the first time in my life that I have heard myself utter a cry of joy. The cry that bursts out when there is a miracle: a beloved person resuscitates after three days of nothingness, for example. The cry is different from all the other cries. It is the cry of victory of the life that comes to reverse death. Never again will I utter such a cry. Unfortunately it is impossible to "give" it to you as it welled up, from the depths of the spiritual body within me whose commands I don't know. So I thought. It is the purest note of any hymn. And when you call, I will give you *the memory of a cry*.

we could continue to send one another Towers, nothing would stop us

I was right not to announce the death of the cat

—There were problems, says my mother. There's no need to destroy cities like that. Everyone has their problems.

No one knows I wept the death of my beloved more than for all the world's towers, more than for the lost children, more than for Rimbaud, all night long I talked to her, I stroked her, time's thread trickles rosé in spite of my pleas, who is still on the bed in pajamas? Thea, the blissful, stroke her for me, I stroke her for Isaac, I don't tell Isaac that Thea has been snatched away from me, I must give her back to Nature, death with its knife takes a slice of my heart, without anesthesia—bon appétit, says my mother, I don't want to spoil her English sauerkraut.

my beloved takes me in her little white velvet arms, with her minuscule mouth she puts a kiss on the kiss of my mouth, when Isaac is traveling, she plays Isaac's role, she takes my life into her body

The two Towers died, the following day, Thea is felled by death, all night I watch over her she watches over me, I don't know in what sleep without sleep I hold her in my arms, and we live each moment of a life that relinquishes itself to death with the regularity of an hourglass, what does one call this life of absolute attachment,

—What time is it? —Three-forty-five in the morning, a bad night, a hurricane of anguish, it's war, outside, within, without exaggerating, without dramatizing, it's a satanic blow to the side, I don't know how I am going to manage. Thea is well? Tell her I'll be back soon—

my beloved meowed to summon me, I look for her, she is at the back of the garden behind the laurel hedge, it is her voice, she is in my arms, an infant with a head wound, I lick the cut, I don't tell Isaac, she is only her name, I am afraid that he will be afraid

And if she were to revive? But already a slender strand of blood beads her mouth where her smile floats tries to float, she sinks into the world of dreams and while the minutes drift away smiles as she deserts her body.

She says: Next year in New York?

He says: Yes.

He says: I remember the first time, the two Towers, the twins, the two of us, a long long time ago, after 1975 but when, I was still using travelers' checks, I remember it very beautiful, very good. But each time that I saw them no sooner settled on the 107th floor than, subliminally, anxiety, I don't speak of this to you

Will I still be able to send cards?

—Yes yes I say. Our tower stays. Montaigne won't cross Ben Laden's mind. Thea blows you a kiss.

She understands everything, Thea.

The television speaks only of that. As if it was over an hour ago, the country is covered in flags

I lost my cap in a taxi, a cap I liked,

but your tie cannot fly away

I think cat, cat, not without cat, a huge veil called Thea spreads slowly over the whole landscape that composes me, over my cities and my lives, and carries her away under my very eyes to the past, all night long the pellets in her bowl drop, one after another, collapse of her kitty litter

When the Towers died, it was my cat I mourned, I tell my daughter, an enduring pain, I feared touching it

I just got back, my mother says, we went to a lecture on painting, always something going on over here I'm going to buy you a pullover I am well fixed for warm clothes because of your blue suit, it's almost my age. We ate a light lunch because this evening we're going to a friend's. Bon appétit!

that the greatest love, the most absolute loves the purest be forever totally unknown

is it her I loved more than anything?

—I'm at Kew Gardens a very nice park, I'm going to see the dahlias. —I'm happy to hear your voice, Mama. —OK, bon appétit, bye.

I don't tell my mother whom I love I hear your voice I am still alive.

She says: Bon appétit. That means *I shall win at the odds.* Do you know the expression? Stop thinking about the Towers.

I nourish my heart on Mama's menus.

I bought some Twin Towers, Isaac says, fetishes, fridge magnets.

They celebrate the reopening of the New York Stock Exchange like the true victory. I dream of my resurrection. Do you think I will be reopened next year in Manhattan? I am still upright. Have to discover the New Restaurant. I didn't tell you: I lost three teeth in two days right in the middle of a poetry reading two teeth plop!, a third behind I could feel wiggle, I put two and two together, the few years that are left are going to be war years, I'm closing in on Ground Zero, I am letting myself be taken by America a blind giant in search of an ant, I don't want to exaggerate, one can't talk only about the end

—Again?! But they've never seen a poet with so many teeth!

—Mandelstam, a true shark. I am going to spend the whole of next year outside the dentist's. I'll write a poem *Lent prochain . . . L'an prochain.* I'll write one called *Ablation.* In fifteen yellow gold Septembers I'll come back, I hope to suffer still and faithful, not having forgotten you when we are ninety and all our false teeth

Still, I'm a little tired, the anxiety about my teeth, for all these gears and springs inside my little body, do you know where the liver is, and the thing they call vesicle?

You have no idea *how ill all's here about my heart,* the uncertainty, the fear, Hamlet to rhyme with effeminate the only difference with Shakespeare is that he took Lexomil that's all

—rock, rock, lullay, I tell myself, in the ghastly Gramercy, the haunted the disquieting Room 624, a grave mix of thoughts, on the king-size bed he says, time, time, 9:11, on his head the kinks are little towers of tarnished silver, and yet Anafranil Lexomil, Morpheus who confuses everything. The notice says: secondary effects impotence troubles of the prostate, I stroked, I licked, I untangled the charms, we undress we want we reach the ageless dateless poisonous organless floor, the Towers are safe, conspiracies exorcised, airplanes soar like angels with their chests freed, lungs full of jubilant notes, we hold each other, but a tower yields, a tower buckles in my mouth I look at the body the forehead in tears of sweat the lovely face that seeks a breath of air in a cloud,

—the death rattle of the cat that suffocates, what is it? a strangler demon, lullay my tiny child, I massage the spine with my heart's prayers I want, I want, I don't know how to give the breath of life to another body,

—do you have the psychic energy? Isaac enquires,

I catch up with life on the edge of the ravine, I bring it back, there is no shore, from the end of its tether it snaps back while we wander on the force's shores seeking a spring a trickle of breath a sigh

I say—yes, I have the psychic energy

I wonder what the psychic energy is, I imagine an electric outlet in the brain, the electricity of the stars, the cat gasps for air, don't think about it, have I the energy, the nerves

I am powerless he says, I am not impotent

—it's not impotence, in his opinion, it's the Towers,

a very gentle kiss, my lips on her tiny pink lips and on my lips the very soft kiss of a mouth the size of a small pink rosebud

I have the psychic energy, I say, I utter the words that temper anxiety, between phantoms and phantasms war is declared, I need the Zen technique that wards off fear, and now and then my verbal pharmacy has therapeutic effects.

—Kiss her for me, Isaac says

I don't say

Let's defy the auguries, I say. Let's ignore the warning about the secondary effects

We talk about the cat, whose secret I keep, I am strangely happy, with
fear, with presentiments of the end, with Mama, with the cat of my
dreams. I am still happy, I am still, we are still, I hear the tiny voice of
my beloved, she is down at the bottom of the Garden of Melancholy,
and I call here I am! I am coming I love you more and more you are
love, you don't stop dying on me, and I write *mourir* like this: *m'ourir*

—if one day in the year 3000 someone discovers all the postcards of
the Towers I have sent you and which one day collapsed, how much
they will have to reconstruct! It was a radiant day, Isaac says.

I am glad the Towers have vanished.

Would they have still been alive with Isaac dead

go on without us?

a bitter flame would have singed my throat, I would never have gone back, but this is not the case, they have been translated to the other side along with you and the cat

This is a thought I can't utter to anyone in the world

Where to put it?

All by itself, between pages 104 and 107.

Without a number.

—What is psychic energy? I ask.

—It's from the American comics, my son says.

—It's sublimated libido, my daughter says.

—Is everything all right? my mother says. I am in the middle of a Pantagruelian meal, there is black rice I thought it was stink bugs and I am drinking a bottle of beaucholais *completely drunk.*

I am full to the gills with leftovers they're bringing a wheelchair to fetch me, the starter was delicious and coming up is apple pie I still have a few of those bugs on my plate and I want to finish this wine

I am not finished, I don't want her to take away my plate

so I'll be back soon and look after yourself

That's my mother, the future past in the present

Translator's Notes

I am grateful to Hélène Cixous for going over parts of the translation with me before it went to press. All errors of omission and/or commission are, of course, my responsibility.

Paris, May 2019

A Note from the Author

Page *x*: here and on two later occasions in the text, 'Morpheus' translates (after consultation with Hélène Cixous) *les morts fées* (the dead fairies), a reference to the fairies and sprites in Shakespeare's *A Midsummer Night's Dream*.

Untitled

Page 2: palace (*palais*). "This is not a precise, realistic place. It can be the king's palace, the *Palais de Justice* (law courts), etc." (HC email, 13 June 2018)

Page 4: *si n'aima*: a literal translation might be "if not love." This is a play on the sound of "cinema" in the previous line.

Page 6: Just before the hunger ends (*Juste avant la fin de la faim*): a play on the sounds of *fin* (end) and *faim* (hunger).

Page 9: the chink in the wall (*l'orée taillée*): "the west window, cut in the stone of Montaigne's study in the Tower, a simple opening, without glass (they used paper)." (HC email, 13 June 2018)

What I Find in Mama's Bottom Drawer

Page 10: "Mama's bottom drawer" is, in French, Mama's *quatrième tiroir* ('fourth drawer'), an allusion to Osip Mandelstam's *Fourth Prose*. I suggested and HC agreed to the "bottom drawer" (the fourth drawer *was* the bottom drawer) as more evocative in English, as, among other things, the place where we put the things we don't use and can't discard.

Page 10: this ordinary Monday: in French *le lundi de l'an général,* which plays on the homophony of *an* (year) and *en* (in general). I found no equivalent in English.

You Never Know Who to Expect

Page 47: Jacques followed his master: *Jacques the Fatalist and His Master* is an eighteenth-century French novel by Denis Diderot, in which, during a journey, a servant, Jacques, is asked by his master to entertain him with stories, but the stories are constantly being interrupted by other characters and their stories. Diderot is believed to have been influenced by Laurence Sterne's digressive novel, *Tristram Shandy.*

Page 51: Your mother is a sage (*Tu as une mère sage*): in French a midwife is a *sage-femme* (wise-woman). Eve Cixous was a midwife by profession.

Page 51: Marcel: Marcel is the name of the handyman and of the handyman's dog. It is also, of course, the first name of the author Marcel Proust and the narrator of his novel, *À la recherche du temps perdu.*

A Letter

Page 65*:* my little Hase: echoes Joachim du Bellay's sonnet (*Les Regrets*): "Happy he who like Ulysses" (Brahic translation):

> Happy he who like Ulysses has made
> A fine voyage, or won the Golden Fleece,
> And returned, full of wisdom and sense,
> To live with his kin the rest of his days.

> When will I see again my little village
> Chimney smoking, and in what season
> The hedges around my modest cottage,
> Which is my province and my heart's reason?

> I prefer the house my ancestors built
> To a Roman palace's grand fronton,
> Better than hard marble I like thin slate:

My Gallic Loire over Tiber's Latin,
My little Liré over Palatine,
Better than sea air, the mild Angevine.

Page 69: it took a Victor Hugo to lead Bacharach instead of Bacharach leading him: In 1840, Hugo visited Bacharach and called it "a sort of Beggars' Headquarters forgotten on the bank of the Rhine by the good taste of Voltaire, by the French Revolution, by the battles of Louis XIV, by the artillery shellings of 1797 and 1805 and by the elegant and wise architects who construct houses in the form of desks and chests of drawers" (*The Rhine*).

Page 72: *Ein Märchen aus alten Zeiten das Kommt mir nicht aus dem Sinn*: "A legend of bygone ages / Haunts me and will not depart" (Heine, "Die Lorelei").

Untitled

Page 86: foolishness: in French *bêtise*, playing on the "beast" in *bêtise*.

Page 88: it even has room for a tower, and more than one: in French, *elle contient même une tour, et plus d'un tour. Une tour* is a tower; "un tour" is a turn, but can also mean a trick; hence, to have more than one trick up one's sleeve.